THE STARTUP SQUAD

FACE THE MUSIC

By Brian Weisfeld and Nicole C. Kear

Imprint
MAKE YOUR MARK

New York

To Mom, for everything
—Brian

For my radical girls, Stella and Valentina
—Nicole

[Imprint]
MAKE YOUR MARK

A part of Macmillan Publishing Group, LLC
120 Broadway, New York, NY 10271

THE STARTUP SQUAD: FACE THE MUSIC. Copyright © 2020 by The Harold Martin Company, LLC.
All rights reserved. Printed in the United States of America by
LSC Communications, Harrisonburg, Virginia.

Library of Congress Cataloging-in-Publication Data is available.

ISBN 978-1-250-18045-2 (hardcover) / ISBN 978-1-250-18046-9 (paperback) /
ISBN 978-1-250-18044-5 (ebook)

Our books may be purchased in bulk for promotional, educational, or business use. Please contact
your local bookseller or the Macmillan Corporate and Premium Sales Department at
(800) 221-7945 ext. 5442 or by email at MacmillanSpecialMarkets@macmillan.com.

Book design by Elynn Cohen

Imprint logo designed by Amanda Spielman

First edition, 2020

1 3 5 7 9 10 8 6 4 2

mackids.com

Also by Brian Weisfeld and Nicole C. Kear

The Startup Squad

Also by Nicole C. Kear

Foreverland

〰〰〰〰〰

The Fix-It Friends series

Have No Fear!

Sticks and Stones

The Show Must Go On

Wish You Were Here

Eyes on the Prize

Three's a Crowd

Jumbo marshmallows.

Where *were* the jumbo marshmallows?

Harriet knelt on her kitchen floor, peering into the depths of the snack cupboard. Her long, dark pigtails grazed the floor as she squinted into the back of the shelves. No marshmallows.

"If I were a jumbo marshmallow, where would I be?" she said to herself as she closed the cabinet and got to her feet. She dusted off the knees of her emerald-green leggings. These always reminded her of *The Wizard of Oz*, which is why she'd paired the leggings with her red gingham farm-girl shirt and a denim miniskirt.

When picking out clothes, most people try to match colors or patterns. Harriet preferred to match themes. On some days, like today, the theme was subtle; on other days, it was so obvious, her outfits resembled costumes. Harriet liked it this way. Clothes should add drama and excitement. Otherwise, what was the point?

"Marshmallows!" she called. "Come out, come out wherever you are!"

Harriet hated silence; whenever she encountered quiet, she broke it. Luckily, her home was rarely quiet—and rarely empty. With a mom whose hair salon was in the basement, an artist dad whose studio was in the garage, and three older brothers—members of a rock band—someone was always around. Today, though, her parents were grocery shopping, her brothers were at a horror movie, and Harriet had stayed home since neither activity held any interest for her. Marshmallows, on the other hand, were of great interest.

Harriet opened the cabinet that held the pots and pans—no luck—and then the one with all the plates and bowls. She did find something wonderful there, but it wasn't the bag of marshmallows. Curled into a salad bowl was her brothers' pet skink, Zappa, sleeping soundly. The pink stretchy headband Harriet had placed over the reptile's head had slipped and was covering her eyes like a sleeping mask.

"Zappa bo bappa," Harriet cooed. She lifted the reptile out of the bowl and cradled her in her arms. Zappa opened her eyes and clambered onto Harriet's shoulder. She clamped her tiny claws onto Harriet's shirt and promptly resumed sleeping.

Harriet was just adjusting the headband on Zappa's head when she heard a knock at the door. She was thrilled. If there was one thing Harriet liked more than visitors, it was surprise visitors.

"*Coming!*" she bellowed, and skipped to the door, clutching Zappa so the skink didn't fall. She looked through the peephole and found her friends Amelia, Didi, and Resa standing on the front steps.

"Hiiiiii!" she cried, flinging open the door.

Resa and Amelia were facing each other, in the middle of a heated debate.

"You're joking, right?" Resa was saying. "The carbon fiber racket is *so* much better than the aluminum! End of discussion."

Amelia shook her head in wonder. "I don't know *why* I thought taking tennis lessons with you might be stressful."

"Come in!" Harriet squealed. "I'm so glad to seeeeeeeee you!"

She clapped her hands, which made Zappa pick up her head and look around before deciding it was nothing worth waking up for. Didi, who'd been standing on the top step, startled at the sight of Zappa's moving, and she would have bolted if Harriet hadn't grabbed her hand just then.

"Don't worry, Didi," said Harriet as she pulled her inside. "I'll keep Zappa out of your hair." She raised her eyebrows way up and nodded quickly. "Get it? Out of your . . . hair? Because of how Zappa got tangled in your hair last time?"

"Uh, yeah, I remember," said Didi nervously. Her long, wavy hair, the color of chestnuts, hung loose around her shoulders and down her back. She gathered it together and shoved it inside her sweatshirt, then pulled the hood up and cinched it closed.

Harriet knew Didi didn't like skinks. Not just skinks, actually, but all reptiles. Not just reptiles, actually, but most animals. Harriet could not fathom this. It was like not liking ice cream or birthdays. Harriet adored animals. Especially the scaly little sucker attached to her shoulder.

"I'm so glad you all are here!" Harriet exclaimed as she led the girls into the small, bright kitchen. "I have been bored out of my gourd! And I can't find the jumbo marshmallows anywhere!" She opened the fridge and peered inside.

"You keep your marshmallows in the fridge?" asked Amelia. She tucked her pale blond hair behind her ears in a gesture that had become such a force of habit she didn't even realize she was doing it.

"No," said Harriet, "but things end up in weird places in this house. Once, I found my hairbrush in here, in the fruit drawer." She closed the fridge and began to search the broom closet.

Resa followed behind her. "We come with exciting news! Harriet, you are not going to believe what we just read in the newspaper."

"Was it a headline that said, 'Marshmallow thief arrested'?" asked Harriet, closing the closet door.

"Uh, no," replied Resa. "It's about your favorite—Harriet, watch out!"

Harriet had clambered onto the kitchen counter and was pulling herself up to standing so she could peek over the top of the cabinets.

Instinctively, Resa put her hands up behind Harriet, spotting her. "You're gonna fall!"

Harriet raised herself up on tiptoe and peeked over the top of the cabinet. "Aha!" Something was there, though it was hard to tell what from a quick glimpse. Steadying herself with one hand, she reached out with the other and closed her fingers around . . . something.

"Bingo!" she exclaimed as she pulled it down. It wasn't the bag of marshmallows, but it was something she'd been looking for.

"Oh, curling iron, how I've missed you!" Harriet said.

She turned to show the girls the treasure she'd uncovered, but the sudden movement threw her off balance. She took a step back and would have fallen off the counter if Resa's hands hadn't been there to shove her back into place. In the hubbub, the curling iron flew out of her hands, hitting Amelia in the arm. Amelia's shriek startled Zappa, and the skink made a run for it, darting down Harriet's body, then down Resa's body, and then onto the kitchen floor.

"Nooooo!" Didi screamed. "Not again!"

She scrambled onto the kitchen table, knocking off books and papers and cereal boxes. She crossed her arms in an X in front of her face, as if she were warding off vampires.

But Zappa wasn't interested in Didi. Instead, she darted over to the thirsty-looking ficus in the corner and dragged something out from behind it with her mouth.

Resa walked over to investigate.

"Looks like Zappa solved the mystery of the missing marshmallows." Resa pulled the bag of jumbo confections from Zappa's mouth. The skink paused for a moment, considering her next move, then padded out of the kitchen.

"Hallelujah!" Harriet exclaimed. She jumped down from the counter with a thud.

"Not so fast!" Resa ordered, holding the marshmallows high above her head. "You'll get these after you listen to our news! Now, sit!"

Harriet lifted her brother's calculus textbook off the nearest chair and sat. She pantomimed zipping her mouth shut.

"You too, Didi," Resa added. "The skink's gone."

Didi squinted open her eyes. "Aren't there more around here?" she asked.

"Yes, but all the other skinks are in cages," said Harriet. "Only Zappa gets to roam free."

Didi carefully climbed off the table but kept her hood pulled tight over her hair.

"So," said Resa. She drum-rolled her toes, clad in Converse per usual—yellow this time. "We were reading the paper, and there was an article about a big Battle of the Bands that's happening at the high school at the end of this month."

"And get this!" Amelia broke in. "The winner of the Battle of the Bands—"

"Gets to be on *American Supahstars!*" Resa announced.

Resa, Didi, and Amelia all watched Harriet's face, bracing themselves for an explosion of joy. Harriet went off like a firecracker over the smallest thing, and this, right here, was genuinely big news.

But Harriet said nothing. Her face was blank and expressionless.

Harriet's face was never blank and expressionless. It was always crowded with feelings—loud, intense, impossible-to-ignore feelings. So Resa tried again.

"The winner," Resa repeated, "is going to be on *American Supahstars!*"

"Yeah," Harriet said. "I read that this morning, too."

Didi pushed her tortoiseshell eyeglasses up her nose. "We thought your brothers might want to enter the Battle of the Bands."

"Right," Harriet replied, nodding.

"We're talking about *American Supahstars*," Resa said, utterly perplexed. "Your favorite show? The one judged by Connor Mackelvoe, who you've written at least six fan letters to . . . Okay, I'm sorry, why are you not freaking out?"

It was true. Harriet loved *American Supahstars*. They all did, though Resa protested she only watched because it was so bad it was good, and Amelia swore she just liked hearing the inventive insults that Connor Mackelvoe hurled at contestants. But Harriet was the show's biggest fan. And here she was not saying a word about the very real possibility that her brothers might appear on it.

Harriet knew she'd have to tell the girls the bad news about her brothers' band, but she really didn't want to. "Can I have the marshmallows now?" she asked. Still puzzled, Resa handed them over, and

Harriet set about constructing a little marshmallow pyramid on the table in front of her.

She sighed heavily. "You're totally right. It would be super cool for my brothers and a dream come true for me. But the band can't be on *American Supahstars*."

"Why not?" asked Didi.

"Because there is no band anymore," Harriet said. She placed a pillowy marshmallow on the very top of the pyramid she'd built.

"The Skinks broke up," she continued. "And it's all my fault."

"The Skinks broke up?" Didi repeated. She was peering out from her cinched-tight hood.

"Wait," said Resa, taking a seat next to Harriet. "I thought your brothers had a whole bunch of different bands—the Rancid Skinks and the Rambling Skinks and . . . others I don't remember."

"They stopped doing those and decided to get really serious about classic rock," said Harriet. "They've been the Radical Skinks for a while."

"Got it," said Amelia, sitting down on the other side of Harriet. "So the Radical Skinks broke up?"

Harriet started constructing another marshmallow pyramid on the table, this one in front of Didi. "Well, the band's not playing together anymore, but it's not because they hate each other." She cast her eyes downward. "It's me they hate. I broke Larry's guitar."

Harriet didn't often feel sad. Angry, yes, frustrated, sure, excited, restless, curious—all the time. But not usually sad. Now, however, she was heavy and low-down, feeling a lump form in her throat. Few things felt as bad as when her brothers were all mad at her.

"What happened?" asked Resa.

"It was an accident! I was chasing Zappa around the living room because she had a chocolate bar in her mouth, and skinks *cannot* eat chocolate. It's like skink kryptonite or whatever." Harriet began making a marshmallow pyramid in front of Resa. "So I didn't see Larry's guitar lying there, and I ran right over it. There was a *craaaaack* sound . . ." Harriet paused for dramatic effect. "And that was the end of Herbert."

"Herbert?" Didi asked.

Harriet nodded. "That was the guitar's name."

"Larry named his guitar?" asked Amelia.

Harriet furrowed her eyebrows. "Of course. Doesn't everybody?"

Resa opened her mouth to reply but thought better of it.

"It took Larry almost a year to save up enough

to buy Herbert," said Harriet. She finished Resa's pyramid and started constructing one in front of Amelia. "By the time he saves up enough for a new guitar, Sam will be graduating and off to college. The band's done for. And it's all my fault."

"So I guess that means no *American Supahstars*," said Amelia, sighing.

"No to *American Supahstars*." Harriet shook her head sadly. "But yes to the chipmunk challenge. Ready, everybody? Begin!"

The girls had no idea what the chipmunk challenge was, but it didn't take long to figure it out. They watched as Harriet tucked one, two, then three marshmallows into her right cheek, making it bulge like an overstuffed suitcase. She repeated the process with her left cheek. She tried to smile, but her cheeks were stretched taut and wouldn't budge.

Amelia could cram only two marshmallows into each of her cheeks. Didi, still nervous about Zappa and not a fan of choking hazards, opted for a single marshmallow on each side. Resa, though, fueled by her competitive zeal, easily stuffed three marshmallows into each cheek and then, while all the girls watched, readied to jam a fourth marshmallow in as well.

Didi shook her head and grabbed it out of Resa's hand, shoving it back into the bag. Even soft, pillowy marshmallows could be dangerous if you weren't careful.

Harriet clapped enthusiastically for Resa. Then she started chewing.

There was a moment of silence as all four girls set about the difficult task of consuming a huge number of jumbo marshmallows, all at once.

"Owmushduh agetacos?" Resa asked, her mouth full.

Didi swallowed, then said, "Sorry, we don't speak Marshmallow."

Resa made a big show of chewing, and chewing, and chewing, then said, "How much does a new guitar cost?"

"Five hundred?" ventured Harriet. "A thousand?" She picked up the curling iron from where it had landed on the table and squeezed it with her hand to open and close its clamp. It looked like the jaws of a shiny metal animal.

"Try one hundred and twenty-five dollars," said Amelia, showing them the results of a quick internet search on her phone.

"We made more than that selling lemonade," remembered Resa. She had a definite glint in her eye. Harriet had only just started to get to know Resa, but Didi, who'd been Resa's best friend since kindergarten, knew exactly what that glint meant.

Resa was getting an idea. And when Resa had

an idea, nothing would stop her until that idea had been fully realized.

"You want to run another lemonade stand?" asked Didi. "To raise money for the Skinks?"

"Nah," said Resa. She readjusted her yellow stretchy headband around her curls. "Lemonade's great and all, but that's small potatoes. I'm thinking of something bigger."

"Big potatoes!" cried Harriet. "I love it." She leaned over her chair to plug the curling iron into the outlet in the wall.

"I'm thinking of something like this," Resa explained, picking up a men's T-shirt that was lying across the back of a kitchen chair. It was black with the words PASTA APOCALYPSE on it and a guitar dripping blood onto a plate of spaghetti.

The girls looked at her, completely lost.

"Are we talking about big potatoes or killer spaghetti? And also, have I entered the Twilight Zone?" Amelia asked.

"Merch!" announced Resa. "What better way to raise money for the Radical Skinks than to sell Radical Skinks merchandise? And who better to do it than the Startup Squad?"

Amelia was biting her lip as she considered. "Merch? You mean, like, Skinks T-shirts?"

"That's exactly what I mean!" said Resa. "Maybe hats, too. The possibilities are endless."

Amelia was nodding. "That actually could work."

Resa raised her eyebrows. "Actually?"

"It's a *great* idea," said Didi. "After all, the Skinks totally saved us when we had our lemonade stand. That concert they put together was amazing."

"And remember how many Skinks fans showed up?" Amelia said. "We were turning people away."

"The Radical Skinks don't just have fans," Harriet said. She clamped the curling iron onto the end of her pigtail and rolled it upward in one deft motion. "The Radical Skinks have megafans. They have fanatics."

"So . . . how would it work?" asked Amelia. She was a fan of big ideas only if they had a lot of small details to hold them up and make them solid. "We'd sell the merch and give the profits to the Radical Skinks for a new guitar? How would we sell it? Where? When?"

Resa frowned. Sometimes Amelia's attention to detail felt like a pin popping her high-flying schemes.

But Harriet didn't mind. The questions got her thinking. "Another show!" she exclaimed. She released her hair from the curling iron, revealing a perfectly corkscrewed lock. "We'll plan a concert at the park. This time, I'll get the right permits—trust me, I learned that the hard way. At the show, we'll sell the merch! That way, not only will the T-shirts make money, but they'll also create buzz!"

"We'd have to do it soon," mused Amelia thoughtfully. "The Battle of the Bands is at the end of the month. There's not much time."

"Oh, there's plenty of time!" Harriet was rolling up her other pigtail in the curling iron. "I work fast. And I know people—" Her dark eyes widened. "Oh! Oh! Oh!"

"Did you burn yourself?" Didi asked with concern.

"Huh? No, it's just I know the perfect place to get T-shirts made!" Harriet replied. "It's this little gift shop that just opened a few blocks down on Walnut Street. It's a terrible location—no foot traffic over there at all."

Harriet hadn't known foot traffic from foot fungus until a few weeks ago, when the four of them launched their lemonade stand. But Harriet was a fast learner and never forgot a face . . . or a name . . . or a charming expression like *foot traffic*.

"The owner is this super-sweet old lady named Lucy," Harriet continued, "and she has the cutest tabby cat she brings to the store—Rambo. He's orange with—oooh!"

"You burned yourself!" Didi winced.

"No, no, I'm just thinking—I should go ask her right now!" Harriet jumped to her feet, forgetting that the curling iron was still wrapped around her pigtail. Its cord was yanked out of the wall.

Didi covered her eyeglasses with her hands. "I can't look."

Harriet erupted into a fit of laughter. "Okay, *that* time I did burn myself a little. But it's okay! Ears recover fast!"

She uncoiled her hair, unleashing a tightly curled ringlet, and tossed the curling iron onto the crowded kitchen table. Then she rushed into the hallway and started rifling through a heap of shoes. "How many T-shirts will we need?"

"But we don't even have a design yet," Amelia called. "Maybe you should slow down there, sister."

Harriet shoved her left foot into a red rain boot, even though it wasn't remotely cloudy outside.

"I live life in the fast lane," she replied. "There's no slowing me down."

High heels, hiking boots, and stinky men's sneakers all flew through the air as Harriet searched for the rain boot's match.

"I can design the logo," offered Didi. "I mean, if you all want."

"Aha!" Harriet bellowed, finding the other boot and jamming her foot into it. She slid on a denim jacket and skipped back into the kitchen.

She grabbed Didi by the shoulders. "Of course you should design the shirt, you artistic genius, you!" Then she spun to face Amelia. "We can figure out all the details later!"

Before any of the girls could reply, she did a little jazz spin, announced, "Harriet, out!" and bounded through the front door.

"Feel free to use the curling iron!" she shouted over her shoulder as the door closed behind her.

There was a moment of stunned silence. Then Amelia picked up the curling iron, turned to Resa and Didi, and asked, "Anyone know how to use this thing?"

The next morning, Harriet was running late for homeroom, as usual. It was one of life's great mysteries how, even though she left herself a whole hour to get ready for school, it never ended up being enough time.

Every day, she'd be 99 percent ready and just about to walk out the door when some problem would come up. Usually, the problem was of the I-can't-find-something-I-desperately-need variety. It might be the hairbrush she was looking for, or her math notebook, or the dark green socks, which were the only socks in the universe she could possibly wear with her argyle sweater. Before she knew it, she'd be super late and would have to run to school at break-neck speed to get there before first period started.

Today, the indispensable item Harriet was missing was the business card Lucy had given her the day before, with all the pricing information for the T-shirts.

Harriet had planned to stay at Lucy's shop for just a few minutes and then run back to update the girls. But Rambo had been in such a playful mood, Harriet lost track of time.

When she'd gotten home, it was almost dinner-time and the other girls were long gone. So she hadn't had a chance to update them on what Lucy said, and she really wanted to do that at homeroom—which started in exactly eleven minutes. She tore through the upstairs in search of the business card.

"Mom, did you see a blue business card anywhere?" she yelled to her mother, who was washing dishes downstairs.

"Did you ever hear the expression 'needle in a haystack'?" came her mom's reply.

"Not helpful, Mom!"

Her mom was right. Finding a small piece of paper in her bedroom was nearly impossible. She was, as her brothers liked to remind her, the luckiest kid in the family since she was the only one with her own room. She didn't have the problem her brothers always complained about: other people always moving their stuff around. But even though she could always count on her belongings being where she left them, she still couldn't find anything in the disaster area that was her bedroom.

She waded through the sea of discarded clothing, which covered her floor. Harriet's outfit-selection process was time-consuming and high-impact. She couldn't tell what she wanted to wear just by looking at the clothes; she needed to try them on. Usually, she had to try on at least five or six items before she found something that worked, and then there was no time to put the clothes back before school.

Today she'd settled on magenta jeans with a black-and-white striped shirt that looked as if it'd come straight off a Venetian gondolier. She'd folded a flowy white scarf to use as a headband, tied it around the back of her neck, and let the ends flow behind her.

She caught a glimpse of herself in the mirror and smiled. It was a really good outfit. All that was missing was a jacket. The denim one with the cool buttons on the front would look super cute. She grabbed it from the corner where she'd thrown it last night, and as she did, a blue piece of card stock fluttered from its pocket.

"Bingo!" she yelled triumphantly. Card in hand, she raced down the stairs, nearly colliding with her brother.

"Larry!" she yelled as she hurried over to the shoe pile to grab her sneakers. "You're not even dressed. You're going to be really late!"

"Calculus problem set." He rubbed the top of his buzzed hair sleepily. "Took me 'til one A.M. to finish."

"Why didn't you just ask what's-her-face?" Harriet asked. "The girl in your class who always helps you?"

"I don't want to, like, *bother* Eleanor all the time," Larry said.

Larry was a big softie. At sixteen, he was the middle of Harriet's three brothers and the one she was closest to. Sam, the oldest, and Joe, the youngest, both treated her like a kid, but Larry listened to her and respected her opinions. It's why she felt especially bad that she'd broken his guitar.

"Well, I'm off to see some girls about getting a new guitar for you!" Harriet grabbed her backpack and slung it over her shoulder. "So you guys better start rehearsing again. I want you ready for the Battle of the Bands this month."

"Oh, wow. Thanks. Yeah, that's—that's totally awesome," said Larry. "Just . . . don't—"

She spun around in the doorway to face him.

"I know, I know!" she said. "I'm not going to get carried away!"

With that, she leaped down the three short steps and raced to school, forgetting to close the door behind her.

wwwww

Harriet made it to school in six and a half minutes, and knocked down only one person in the process. She was breathing hard when she hurried into Ms. Davis's room, with four whole minutes left of homeroom.

"Hey!" she panted, beelining over to the table where Amelia, Didi, and Resa sat.

"Harriet," came Ms. Davis's stern voice from the front of the room. "How many times have I told you to slow down?"

Harriet turned to look at Ms. Davis. "What can I say? I live life in the fast lane."

"Not in here you don't," Ms. Davis shot back. "In my classroom, you stay below the speed limit."

Harriet flashed Ms. Davis a 100-watt smile. "Sorry! I'll take it down a notch."

"Let's make it three notches," said Ms. Davis, peering at Harriet over the top of her eyeglasses. Harriet had learned from experience that arguing with stubborn Ms. Davis was pointless. Ms. Davis really cared about having the last word, so Harriet let her have it, even when she didn't fully agree.

Harriet walked briskly to the girls, pulling Lucy's business card out of her pocket and slamming it down on the table.

"Voilà!" she announced.

Amelia scrunched her nose up in confusion. "One pack of sardines and a chicken liver?"

Harriet giggled. "Oops, wrong side." She flipped the business card over. "That was a recipe for Rambo's favorite cat treats. Here's the important stuff."

"Fifteen dollars each . . . if under one hundred fifty . . . Is this from Lucy?" Didi asked.

Harriet slid into the seat next to Didi. "It's all figured out!" she announced with pride. "Lucy was super into it!"

"How long will it take to make the shirts?" Resa asked.

"About two to three weeks," Harriet said.

Resa's shoulders slumped. "But that won't work. The Battle of the Bands is in three weeks! We need to have the fund-raising show soon."

"I know," said Harriet with a satisfied smile. "That's why I asked her to rush the order."

"She can do that?" asked Resa skeptically.

"Sure," said Harriet. "I told you, we're pals."

"And it won't cost extra?" asked Didi.

"Well, yeah, a *little* extra, but just . . ." Harriet

glanced down at the business card. "Just five dollars more a shirt."

"So it's really twenty dollars each shirt."

"Less, if we order more than one hundred and fifty," said Harriet.

"We're not going to sell more than one hundred and fifty T-shirts," said Resa. "Not even to Skinks fanatics."

"Still, it's a good price," Harriet said. "I'd pay twenty dollars for a T-shirt if I loved the band."

"If we buy them for twenty dollars, we can't sell them for twenty dollars," said Amelia. "Or we won't make any money."

"Oh *right*," said Harriet.

"We'd need to mark up the price by a few bucks." Amelia scribbled numbers in her notebook. "Do you think we can sell twenty-five shirts?"

There were murmurs of agreement.

"So, if we sell twenty-five T-shirts and charge twenty-three dollars each, we'd make seventy-five dollars." Amelia looked up at them. "It's probably better to charge twenty-five dollars—that'll give us a profit of one hundred and twenty-five dollars, enough for a new guitar." She twiddled her pencil rapidly between her fingers. "Is twenty-five dollars too much for a T-shirt?"

"Yes!" said Resa at the exact same time Harriet said, "No!"

"Didi?" asked Amelia. "Want to be the tiebreaker?"

Didi did not want to be the tiebreaker. She hated getting in the middle of arguments and taking sides. She gnawed on her thumbnail as she considered a reply that wouldn't get her in trouble with either girl. "It's not a ridiculous price," she said. "But it is a little high. Could we maybe—I mean, have we looked for a better deal online?"

"But it's already set up!" Harriet protested.

"I did poke around a bit last night," said Amelia, "and the trouble with online shops is a lot of them have high minimum orders. Over one hundred T-shirts at least."

"See? Lucy's deal is better. We can order just twenty-five T-shirts, and if each costs twenty dollars, then all we need is . . ."

Harriet squinted one eye closed and then the other. She stuck her tongue out to the side. She made faint buzzing sounds.

"What's she doing?" whispered Didi to Amelia.

"Math, I think?" Amelia whispered back.

"Five hundred dollars!" announced Harriet. "We need only five hundred dollars to place the order."

"Waaaaaaaait a second," said Resa, holding her hand up. "She needs the money up front?"

"People usually do," said Amelia.

"We don't have five hundred dollars!" Resa exclaimed. The whole thing was becoming a lot more complicated than she'd imagined.

"I have a little money saved," Didi offered. "I've been saving for this acrylic paint set. There's four shades of blue—indigo, azure, turquoise, and cerulean. I have about thirty-one dollars."

Resa put her hand on Didi's arm. "For the love of Pete, you can keep your cerulean, you big color nerd. You don't have nearly enough anyway."

"Why don't we just do preorders?" asked Amelia. "Make people pay for the T-shirts beforehand, and use that money to place the order?"

"Your backhand is awful," said Resa. "But your ideas aren't half-bad."

"How did I not see this headache coming when I signed up for tennis with you?" Amelia muttered to herself. "How?"

The bell rang, signaling the end of homeroom. Harriet jumped out of her seat, with Amelia right behind her. The two of them had Mrs. Ross for science first period, and she made Ms. Davis look like a cuddly teddy bear. If you were even a minute late, you had to recite the entire periodic table.

"Meet at my house after school?" asked Harriet over her shoulder.

"Tennis," Amelia and Resa said in unison.

"And trust me," added Resa, "she can't afford to miss a lesson."

"Come after tennis, then! For dinner!" Harriet said. "I'm cooking!"

Before any of the girls could reply, she yanked on Amelia's hand and pulled her into the sea of middle schoolers on their way to first period.

When Amelia and Resa arrived at Harriet's house, still sweaty from tennis, they found the front door ajar. The unmistakable sound of a drum solo emanated from the second floor. Someone was whaling on their drums, culminating in a cataclysm of cymbals.

"Should we go in?" asked Resa warily.

"I'd knock first," said Amelia, "but somehow I don't think anyone would hear it."

"Fair enough," replied Resa. "So go ahead."

"You first."

"Why me?"

"This whole thing was your idea," Amelia pointed out. "Plus, I beat you at sprints in warm-ups."

"Only because you got a head start!" Resa protested.

But Amelia was already pushing her inside.

"Harriet?" Resa called, and then more loudly, "Haaaaarriet?"

"*In here!*" came Harriet's voice from the kitchen.

Amelia and Resa walked carefully down the narrow hallway, paying special attention to where they placed their feet. They'd learned from experience that skinks could be anywhere in the Nguyen household.

Didi was standing at the kitchen sink, holding a green colander and looking nervous. She wore a knit winter hat pulled low over her forehead. Not one tendril of hair escaped from the hat.

"Nice skink armor," Resa said, nodding at the hat.

"Fool me once . . ." replied Didi.

Harriet stood at the stove top, grunting as she stirred a steaming pot, which was almost half her size. She'd moved the white see-through scarf onto her ponytail and rolled up the sleeves of her gondolier shirt.

Amelia and Resa laid their backpacks and racket bags down and walked over to investigate. Huge plumes of steam billowed over Harriet's face as she stirred. She inhaled deeply. "Great for the complexion!" she said. "Want to try?"

"I'm good," said Amelia.

"Got enough pasta in there?" asked Resa.

Harriet bit her lip, looking concerned. "I think so. I mean, I used four boxes."

Resa laughed. "I was kidding, Harriet. That's the biggest pot I've ever seen—and my mom is a professional baker. How many people are you feeding?"

Harriet wiped sweat from her upper lip with the back of her hand. "My mom's with a client downstairs, but she might eat some later. Dad's working on a sculpture. For now, it's just you all and my brothers. But you've never seen my brothers eat—especially my famous mac 'n' mystery cheese."

Harriet pulled the wooden spoon out of the pot and handed it to Amelia. "Can you take over for a minute?"

Amelia obliged, and Harriet headed to the fridge, where she rifled through the crowded shelves.

"Who taught you to cook?" asked Resa.

"Oh, I'm self-taught," said Harriet over her shoulder. "My mom usually works nights at the salon, and my brothers are hopeless. They'll crack open a super-size bag of potato chips and call it dinner. My dad can cook, but if he's working on a painting or a sculpture, all hope is lost. He'll completely forget to eat."

Harriet found what she was looking for in the fridge—an orange hunk of cheddar and a Ziploc bag containing some kind of crumbled white cheese. "Heads up, Didi!" she announced as she chucked the cheeses at her.

Didi caught them both in the colander. "Hey, we just invented cheeseball!" She giggled as she looked at the food she'd caught. "This is cheddar, but . . . what's this one?"

"I think that's the mystery cheese," Amelia chimed in.

It took the girls a while to figure out how to drain the super-size pasta pot, and there was a mini-disaster when Zappa ambled in and Didi panicked and dropped a gallon of milk. But eventually, Zappa was apprehended, the milk was cleaned up, and dinner was served.

"*Joe! Sam! Laaaaaaaaaaarry!*" Harriet bellowed, trying to be heard over the sound of drums. "*Food!*" She stood at the kitchen table, spooning mystery macaroni into mismatched bowls.

The sound of drums was replaced by thunderous pounding on the stairs. A few seconds later, the Nguyen brothers rushed into the room.

Joe was the shortest of the bunch, but his hair was

the longest by far. It hung down to his shoulders, covering one side of his face. When he sang, it gave him a brooding, mysterious look that his fans loved. Sam, the oldest, had a neat, classic haircut, with plenty of hair gel to keep it slicked into place. This, paired with his black rectangular glasses, made him look like a young businessman, though his T-shirt—bloodred with the words PANIC AT THE JUNKYARD on it—made it clear he was a rock and roller. Larry loomed over his brothers, so tall and thin that Harriet sometimes teasingly called him Larry the Scary-crow.

"Sam, the drums are sounding great," said Harriet with a smile.

"Thanks, Harry," said Sam. "What'd you make tonight?"

"Please don't say hamburger-a-bob," pleaded Joe.

"I like hamburger-a-bob," protested Larry.

"Yeah," said Joe. "But you have no standards."

"I made mac 'n' mystery cheese!" announced Harriet.

There was collective whooping as the boys grabbed bowls of food. Joe and Sam nabbed seats and started shoveling big spoonfuls into their mouths. Larry, ever thoughtful, dragged over extra chairs for the guests.

"You guys remember my business associates, right?" Harriet asked her brothers. She gestured to each girl as she named them. "Amelia, Didi, and Resa."

"Hey, we want to thank you ladies," said Larry. "It's really cool of you to help us."

"No problem," said Resa. "After all, you guys helped us when we had our lemonade stand."

"Plus," said Amelia, "it would be mind-blowing to personally know one of the acts on *American Supahstars*." She took a small, careful bite of the macaroni, bracing herself for something truly revolting. Instead, she was surprised to find that while the pasta was a little dry and bland, it was pretty good. Definitely not terrible. Which was more than anyone could say about her own cooking.

"Does it upset anyone else that they misspelled *superstars*?" Didi asked.

"They do that on purpose," said Resa.

"Yeah, to trademark it," Sam agreed. "Now they own that word."

"Really?" asked Didi, adding some Parmesan to her food. "You can own a word?"

"Yeah, for sure," said Sam. "That's what it means when you see the little *TM* or *R* next to stuff. People can use the word *superstars*, but no one can use the word *supahstars* without paying them."

"Smart," observed Amelia. "But shouldn't it really be *supahstahs*?"

"Ha!" said Harriet. "Yes!"

"So," said Joe, pushing his empty bowl away and leaning back in his chair, "what can we do to help sell the merch? What do you need from us?"

"You just need to get the word out to your fans," said Resa. "Like you did with the lemonade concert."

Joe and Sam pulled cell phones from their pockets and started tapping and swiping at super speed.

"So," started Resa, "if you could post something—"

"Done," said Sam, placing his phone on the table next to his bowl.

"We've got"—Joe swiped at his phone—"thirteen . . . no, seventeen . . . hold on, twenty—who can keep up? We've got a lot of likes."

Sam's phone was dinging continuously and vibrating so much it was about to fall off the table. He picked it up and read the alerts. "Skinks 4Eva is freaking out. They're begging us for deets." He scrolled down on his screen and smiled.

Harriet sighed. It felt as if her brothers were glued to their phones most of the time—except Larry, who couldn't keep a phone for longer than a week before he broke it or lost it. After the second replacement, their mom said he could get another phone just as soon as he could buy it himself.

Harriet had been begging for a phone for what

felt like forever, but her mom wouldn't budge: Harriet would have to wait until she was in high school. Her mom said it costs too much and liked to throw around the term *digital zombies*, but Harriet suspected part of the reason was she wanted her baby to be a baby for as long as possible.

"We have momentum," observed Sam. "We should follow up right now with details."

"We don't even have a logo yet," protested Didi. "I mean, I've been working on one, but—"

Joe waved his hand in the air. "We don't need a logo to sell these shirts. Our fans will buy 'em sight unseen."

"We just have to tell them how much, and who to give the money to," said Sam.

"We were thinking," said Amelia, "twenty-five dollars a shirt?"

Sam and Joe tapped a few keys, and instantly their phones started dinging and buzzing again.

Harriet was happy to see all her favorite people gathered around a table, working together. Didi, though, did not look happy. She was nibbling on her thumbnail, and she'd hardly touched her food.

"What's the matter, Di?" asked Harriet.

"It's just . . . that's a lot of money," Didi said. "What if people don't like the design?"

"Fear not!" Harriet said, putting an arm around Didi's shoulders. "Everyone's going to love it. You're the next Vincent van Gogh! Just, you know, with both your ears."

Didi turned to the boys. "You guys should probably look at the logos I'm working—"

Joe stood. "For sure," he said. "But right now, we gotta practice." His phone buzzed again, and he looked at it. "People wanna know who to give the money to."

"Me!" announced Harriet. "Tell them I'll be in front of the high school every day this week at three fifteen. They know who I am."

"Everybody knows who Harry is," Sam agreed, ruffling the top of her head like she was a Labrador retriever.

"The hair!" Harriet protested, batting his hand away. She acted annoyed, but really nothing made her happier than when her brothers mussed her hair. The boys were always so busy with calculus and band practice and after-school jobs and the constant buzzing of their phones. She was thrilled to have their attention and their thanks.

"Oh, we wouldn't want to mess up your precious, precious hair," teased Joe. He reached over suddenly and put her in a headlock.

Didi, an only child, shot Harriet a concerned look. "Ummm—that looks . . . I mean . . . Hey, don't hurt her . . ."

But Harriet was laughing hard, belly laughs

that made it tough for Joe to get a handle on her. "Don't worry, Di, my dear," she panted in between guffaws. "They don't call me Harry Houdini for nothing."

And then, in one swift motion, Harriet slipped out of the headlock and kicked Joe's leg out from underneath him. He went tumbling to the floor.

"She schooled you!" Sam laughed.

Joe stood with a proud smile. "She always does."

Larry grabbed a yellow apron from a hook on the wall and slipped it over his head. It was covered in small pink roses and had a heart-shaped pocket on the chest. "You girls relax," he said as he walked to the sink. "I'll get the dishes."

"We can work on the logo," Didi suggested to the others.

"We coooooooould," Harriet said, glancing up at the clock. "But it's almost eight, and you know what that means!"

"Oooooh, *American Supahstars*," said Resa. "Perfect. We can chill *and* do research at the same time. I love multitasking!"

"Yeah, but . . ." Didi started as Harriet threw her arm around Didi's shoulders.

"You and I have been working over a hot stove all day," she said.

Didi shrugged. "It wasn't really all—"

"You know what they say," Harriet said sternly,

leading her down the hallway toward the television in the living room. "All work and no play—"

"Makes Jerry a dull boy," Larry called from the sink.

"Jerry?" asked Didi. "Isn't it Jack?"

Harriet smiled. "Oh, that's just Larry. A genius on the guitar but hopeless with names."

The next morning, Harriet strutted through the door of homeroom in a purple pleather motorcycle jacket with lilac leggings. She spun around, unfolding her collar so that it stuck up.

"My purple power suit," she said to the other girls, raising one eyebrow. "I figured if we mean business, we should look like it. Today's my first day of collecting money for preorders at the high school."

"Is that jacket from your cousin?" Amelia asked. "It has Cam-Thu written all over it."

"Yep," said Harriet, doing a little spin in place.

Resa was intently looking at Didi's sketchbook, which was splayed open on the table in front of her. She was frowning. Didi didn't look too happy, either; she was nibbling on her thumbnail, looking like she was wound tighter than a jack-in-the-box.

Harriet plopped into a chair next to Resa. "What're we looking at?"

"The logos I drew," said Didi. "But nobody likes them."

"Come on, Didi." Resa tipped her chin down and looked at her friend. "You know that's not true."

Amelia jumped in. "Of course we like them. They just need some tweaks."

Harriet pulled the sketchbook toward her. It was open to a black-and-white pencil drawing of an animal that Harriet guessed was supposed to be a skink, even though it looked more like some kind of dinosaur. THE RADICAL SKINKS was written in block letters inside the animal's body, but the letters were so small that it was nearly impossible to read.

"I know, I know, the letters are too small," said Didi, yanking down both sleeves so that they covered her hands. She was trying to stop biting her fingernails.

"Yeah, sort of," said Harriet. "And, uh, the skink . . ."

". . . looks like Godzilla," Resa said.

"Resa!" Amelia scolded. "A little tact!"

"What?" Resa shot back. "It's an *amazing* Godzilla! That's what I'm saying."

Harriet flipped the page to a sheet marked *Option 2*, which featured a circle, inside of which THE RADICAL SKINKS was written in a flowery script.

"I like that one," said Amelia. "Simple. Classic."

Resa snorted. "It's too cute. This is a rock band, not a preschool."

Harriet flipped to the next page, marked *Option 3*. This featured, simply, an enormous *S*, with the word RADICAL written around it in an arc.

"See, this one I like!" Resa exclaimed. "It's bold. Eye-catching!"

"Ummm, it's basically just the Superman logo," Amelia pointed out. "With a random adjective on the top."

Didi shut the sketchbook in exasperation and put it in her backpack.

Harriet could tell she was upset, even though she was trying to be a good sport. "Didi, they're all great!" Harriet offered with a bright smile. "But do you think we could add some color?"

Didi sighed. "Yeah, of course. I just didn't get to that part yet. I'm not stupid."

All three girls, realizing they'd gone too far in their criticisms, talked at once, assuring Didi that no one thought she was stupid. Before she could reply, the bell rang.

Usually Didi, whose next period was English in the room right next door, was one of the last to leave homeroom. Today, she was out the door like a bullet.

Amelia looked at Harriet and Resa. "That did not go well," she observed.

"I'll cheer her up at lunch! I brought cookies!" Harriet promised as she wove through the crowd to get to the door. Science waited for no one.

But Didi didn't come down to the cafeteria for lunch. Resa explained that Didi had gone to the art studio to help Mr. Ewoja sharpen the colored pencils. It settled her nerves.

The next morning, Didi came to school late, at the very end of homeroom, and spent lunch cleaning paintbrushes for Mr. Ewoja.

"Doggonit," said Harriet, shaking salt onto her hot lunch: pasta with vegetables. "I brought her marshmallows today. No one can be sad when they're doing the chipmunk challenge."

Amelia was mixing a carton of Greek yogurt into a Tupperware full of fruit. "Maybe we should go find her in the art studio," she suggested.

Resa looked at Amelia for a second, waiting for her to catch her mistake.

"Harriet can't go to the art studio," said Resa. "She's been banned."

"Banned? Are you kidding?" asked Amelia.

"I keep forgetting you got here only a few months ago," said Resa, taking a bite of her hummus-and-shaved-carrots sandwich, one of her mom's creations. "You weren't here for Glittergate."

"That sounds like something not to be missed," said Amelia.

"It wasn't that big of a deal," Harriet said. Glittergate was one of those stories that refused to go away, and though it wasn't the most embarrassing thing she'd ever done—in fact, it didn't even rank in the top five—she was still hoping it would eventually disappear from everyone's memory.

"So we were in fourth grade, making these Day of the Dead masks in art," said Resa, ignoring Harriet's expression. "Mr. Ewoja had the glitter out for us to use——"

"Who doesn't love glitter?" Amelia asked, smiling.

"Yes! Exactly! Everyone loves glitter!" agreed Harriet. "Could've happened to anyone!"

"Clyde McGovern was using the red glitter for his mask, and you know him—he'll do anything for a laugh," Resa said, pausing to take a sip of milk. "So he shook the bottle of glitter and sprinkled a little over his head."

"So I did, too, and that's the whole story," Harriet broke in.

"Right—except Harriet's bottle wasn't opened to

the sprinkle setting; it was just completely open—wiiiiiide open . . ." Resa started chuckling.

"Oh no," said Amelia, eyes wide with delighted horror.

"And the whole bottle of glitter dumped out onto her head!" Resa finished.

"The thing about glitter," said Harriet reflectively, "is that it can really travel."

"It went *everywhere*," said Resa, laughing. "The more she tried to get it out of her hair, the more it flew everywhere. It was like being inside a snow globe."

"Awww, that sounds kind of nice, actually," said Amelia. She scooped up a large piece of cantaloupe with yogurt.

Harriet's face brightened. "I thought so, too! Mr. Ewoja, not so much."

"He banned her from the art studio," Resa said. She took a bite of her sandwich, having concluded her story.

"It's a bummer. I'm dying to tell Didi how many preorders we got yesterday," said Harriet. "I knew there'd be a lot, but sixteen? Already?"

"I can hear those guitar chords!" said Resa.

"The hardest part was getting the first few people to buy," said Harriet, shaking a carrot off her fork so that it held only pasta. "Once there was a little crowd around me, people walking by came over to see what was going on. FOMO comes in handy sometimes."

"You're a master salesperson," said Amelia with admiration. "You've got serious skills."

"Thank you, thank you." Beaming, Harriet pushed peas, broccoli, and carrots around on her plate, searching for any pasta she might have missed. When she'd asked Joan, the woman who served food in the cafeteria, for lunch, she'd said, "Pasta with veggies and hold the veggies." For some reason, Joan had not obliged.

"Can you believe that some people are buying more than one shirt?" Harriet asked. "Reginald Hargrove bought eight! And a bunch of people said they didn't have money but would bring it today, so when I go back to the high school, I'll probably get tons of more orders."

"Didi will be psyched," agreed Resa.

"Maybe I'll check on her tonight, after tennis," said Amelia, snapping the lid on the now-empty Tupperware. "She lives right around the corner from me. I can tell her the good news."

"Good idea," agreed Resa. "After I beat you in tennis, I'll go with you."

"You know what they say about counting your chickens before they hatch," replied Amelia with eyebrows raised.

"Sure," replied Resa, "but chickens are famously

unreliable. And my backhand is anything but. My backhand is foolproof." She crumpled her aluminum foil into a tight ball, then pitched it toward the over-size garbage can a few feet away. It sailed directly in. She turned to Amelia. "I rest my case."

"I'll come to Didi's, too!" said Harriet. "Cam-Thu gave me this adorable dress I want to give her. It has tiny blue tulips all over it."

"That'll put a smile on her face," said Resa. "Didi's never met a floral pattern she doesn't like."

"Meet us at five thirty at Didi's house?" asked Amelia.

"With bells on," said Harriet.

"Bells are fine," said Resa with a wry smile. "Just no glitter."

Harriet was running late, as usual. It didn't help that she couldn't remember Didi's exact address. She'd never been to Didi's house before, and even though she'd made sure to ask Resa for the address, and to write it down on a scrap of paper, she'd left the paper at school.

The address was definitely on Chestnut Street, and it definitely had a four and a seven in it. She just couldn't remember which combination of fours and sevens it was. She tried 447 Chestnut, but no one was home. Then she tried 477 Chestnut, but an old man answered the door and had never heard of

Didi. Now she was headed to 474 and really hoped this was it.

She made a mental note to tell her mother this story as proof that she desperately, urgently, *immediately* needed a cell phone. "For *safety*," she'd say. Or maybe, even better, "It's a matter of public safety." That sounded convincing.

Her mother would almost definitely tell her she should have just remembered to take the paper with the address, silly girl. It was a long shot, but that did not dissuade Harriet. Harriet was a firm believer in the long shot.

She passed 470 Chestnut, then 472. She quickened her step as she approached 474. The lights were on in the front windows—that was a good sign. She walked up the wide steps leading to the dark wooden door. She rang the doorbell.

There was laughter, then footsteps, and then, in the front window, the curtains were pushed back and Didi's face appeared.

"Hallelujah!" exclaimed Harriet as Didi opened the door. She flung her arms around her friend. "It's you!"

Didi laughed. "Were you expecting someone else? I do live here, after all."

Harriet kicked off her shoes at the door and tossed her blue jacket on top of them. Didi couldn't help picking up the jacket and hanging it in the closet, then lining up the shoes neatly, next to the other carefully placed pairs.

"Oh! I brought you something!" said Harriet, pulling the flower-print dress from her backpack. "Courtesy of Cam-Thu."

Didi's face lit up. "Tulips, my favorite! Thank you!"

"So this is Casa Singh!" said Harriet, skipping through the foyer and the living room, into the dining room, where Resa and Amelia were seated at a rectangular wooden table, scrutinizing sketches.

"Ooooh, a glass menagerie!" Harriet cooed, rushing to a set of shelves over a sideboard. There was a whole shelf of tiny glass animals—little birds and elephants and horses, all of them glittering under the light of the dining room. Harriet picked up the largest one—a cat—and placed it in her palm. "I looooove these."

Didi hurried over and hovered close by. "Yeah, they're my mom's. So, um, just be careful because, you know, they're fragile."

Harriet whispered, "Oh yeah, definitely, of course." She lifted her hand up so that the cat caught the light and twinkled like a star.

"Here." Didi reached into Harriet's palm and retrieved the cat gingerly. "I'll just put it back since I know where it goes."

Harriet's feelings were a little hurt. You pour one

bottle of glitter on your head and no one trusts you ever again. Still, she knew Didi didn't mean to hurt her feelings. Didi just liked things neat and tidy and careful, and Harriet lived life in the fast lane, which was messy and thrilling and sometimes involved broken glass. So she decided to let it go.

"Your home is magnificent!" she declared, turning herself in a circle for a panoramic view. "Ooooooh! Who is this handsome devil?" Harriet rushed over to the other side of the room, where a large, round fishbowl sat on a small table. Inside, an electric-blue fish, with long fins fluttering like scarves, swam slowly.

"Oh, that's Beethoven," said Didi. She sprinkled in a pinch of fish food, and Beethoven darted to the surface, attacking the tiny flakes of food with his mouth.

"Ooooh I get it!" said Harriet. "Beethoven, the beta fish!"

"So Harriet," called Resa from the table, "we were just telling Didi about how the T-shirts are selling like hotcakes. What's the update? Did you sell more today?"

Harriet tossed her backpack onto the table and sat down on a high-backed chair. "Did I sell more today? Uhhh, do fish swim? Do birds fly? Are mealworms a skink's favorite food?"

"I'm guessing the answer is yes?" ventured Amelia.

"The answer is abso-stinking-lutely! The answer is without a doubt! We are *swimming* in money! We're going to need a life raft to save us from drowning in the ocean of money we have!" Harriet leaned back in her chair to let the good news soak in.

Didi beamed, and Harriet was glad. Didi was a new-ish friend, but Harriet liked her a lot. Didi was exceedingly eager to help and easy to please.

"What does that mean exactly?" asked Resa, who was less easy to please. "How many preorders do we have?"

Harriet unzipped her backpack and pulled out a spiral notebook. She flipped through the pages, trying to find the preorder information. "Here it is!" she exclaimed, smoothing down a page with a column of numbers. She looked at the bottom of the column, to the total. "One thousand four hundred twenty-three!" she announced. Then, she added a bit nervously, "Wow, that's a lot more than I remember."

Didi pushed her eyeglasses up, squinting as she tried to be diplomatic. "Ummm, Harriet, I don't think that's the right number."

Harriet took another look and broke out giggling. "Oh, this is my math homework. Maybe I shouldn't have written the orders in my math notebook."

Resa raised her eyebrows but held her tongue.

"Don't worry," said Harriet. "It's in here somewhere." She flipped to the last page of the notebook and there—aha!—was the information she needed. It said *preorders* right on the top. Why, then, were only five names written underneath? She'd taken a lot more orders than this.

Harriet flipped the page and looked at the back cover of her notebook.

"Here we go," she said. "I made a mark for each order. And there's . . . twenty-four marks. So we sold twenty-four T-shirts!"

"Harriet, that's amazing," said Didi.

"If we make five dollars on each, that's one hundred and twenty bucks," added Amelia.

"Yes! Approximately," said Harriet. She pulled the hair tie out of her high ponytail, which was starting to give her a headache.

"Why approximately?" asked Resa. "Why not exactly?"

"Well, I mean, we won't make five dollars on all of them. Because of the bulk discount and stuff," Harriet explained. She raked her fingers through her hair to comb it.

"What bulk discount?" asked Resa. She'd crossed her arms over her chest and looked as if she might start yelling at any minute.

"Well, remember how I said Reginald Hargrove bought eight T-shirts?" asked Harriet. "I gave him a bulk discount. That's how I got him to buy eight."

"Ohhhkay," said Amelia. "That makes sense. But how much of a discount did you give him?"

"Half price," said Harriet.

Then came the yelling, right on cue.

"Half price?" Resa exploded. "That's $12.50 each shirt! It costs us twenty dollars with the rush fee. That means we're losing money!"

"But I sold eight of them!" Harriet protested. She was starting to worry she'd made a big mistake.

"Perfect! That means we lost money on a third of all the T-shirts we sold!" Resa yanked her green headband down off her forehead and shoved it back in place.

Now it was Harriet's turn to cross her arms over her chest and glower.

"I think what Resa means," Didi jumped in tactfully, "is that we just want to make these decisions together."

"Please," Harriet snorted. She could read between the lines. "What you really mean is that you want to make all the decisions while I do your dirty work."

"I thought you liked selling the T-shirts," said Amelia.

"I do!" Harriet exclaimed. "I love that part, but I also like having a say in the decisions. And sometimes I need to think on my feet. Stuff comes up!"

"That's true," Didi pointed out to the others. She hated it when they fought and wanted to call a truce as soon as possible. "And a bulk discount is a great idea!"

"Right, but it should be more like ten or fifteen percent off," said Amelia, who was scribbling numbers on a blank page in Harriet's notebook. "If we subtract the money that we're losing on that half-price order, we've made . . ." She winced, looking at the number. "Twenty dollars so far."

"You have got to be kidding me," Resa muttered.

"I get it! I ruin everything!" Harriet lamented. She slumped in her chair and let her hair fall in front of her face.

"People, relax," said Amelia. "We can fix it."

"How?" asked Harriet. "I already collected Reginald's money!"

Didi bit her fingernails. "Maybe we should just leave it."

"We'll catch him in front of the high school tomorrow," said Amelia firmly. "We'll just explain there was a mistake, that the shirts are actually twenty dollars each. That's still a twenty-five percent discount."

"We won't make any money off those shirts at all!" Resa protested.

"Yeah," said Amelia. "But we won't lose any money, either. And maybe he'll tell his friends and get us some word of mouth. It's the best we can do."

"I guess I can do that," Harriet replied, still pouting. "But I'm going to tell him it's your fault!"

"I'm good with that," said Amelia, slipping her pencil behind her ear. "Throw me under the bus."

"If you say so," Harriet said, shrugging.

"Just give me the list of your orders and I'll tally the sizes and type it all up for Lucy. That way, she knows how many sizes of each T-shirt to order."

Harriet handed over the notebook, and Amelia read over the page marked *preorders*.

"Harriet," she said, her voice betraying her worry, "there's only, like, five names here. And no sizes."

"Yeah," confessed Harriet. "On the first day, I forgot to get sizes. But today, I made sure to ask. Turn the page; the sizes are on the back."

Resa opened her mouth to say something, but a sharp glance from Didi made her clamp her mouth closed. She couldn't prevent a loud sigh from escaping, though.

Amelia bit her lip as she read. "Children's large . . . men's extra extra large . . . women's size six?" Amelia looked up at Harriet. "I figured we'd stick to adult sizes. You know, unisex small, medium, large. Keep it simple?"

"*Now* you tell me!" Harriet huffed. "Do I look like a mind reader to you? Do I have a crystal ball?"

Resa could control herself no longer. "Did you even ask Lucy if the T-shirts come in kids' sizes? And what's a six? Is that a medium? A large? Or is six the number of dollars we'll have left when this mess is cleaned up?" She stood abruptly, her chair almost falling to the floor.

"I gotta cool off," she announced. "I'm going for a run around the block."

"Good idea," said Didi. She knew that Resa was trying to be patient and that it wasn't easy.

Resa grabbed her green cardigan and jogged out the front door, which closed loudly behind her.

The sound caught the attention of Didi's mother. "Did someone arrive?" Mrs. Singh stood in the doorway, drying her hands on a dish towel. She was a small woman—short and thin, with delicate features, nothing like Harriet's own mother, who was round-faced, with oversize eyes, mouth, and nose. With her tortoiseshell glasses and long, wavy brown hair, Mrs. Singh bore a striking resemblance to Didi.

"No, Mom," said Didi. "Resa just ran out for a minute. She'll be right back."

Mrs. Singh's face clouded over with concern. "Where could she be going?" she asked. "At this hour?"

Didi smiled. "Mom, it's only six o'clock." She was trying to put her mother at ease, but as usual, it backfired.

"Yes, Indira," her mother said firmly. "But it's getting dark soon. I don't like Resa walking around after dark by herself. It's not safe."

"Okay, Mom," said Didi, suppressing a sigh. "I'll text her and make sure she's all right."

"Please do," her mother said. Then, noticing Harriet for the first time, she smiled brightly. "Hello. Have we met?"

"No, Mrs. Singh!" Harriet got up from the table and did a small curtsy, which made Didi's mom laugh. "I'm Harriet. Enchanted, I'm sure."

"Are you staying for dinner? You are all welcome." Mrs. Singh looked from Harriet to Amelia warmly. "It's only spaghetti, but I have a whole tray of samosas left over from my nephew's birthday party last night. If you put them in the microwave for a few seconds, they are delicious."

"I can't stay," said Harriet apologetically. "My mom is working late, and if I don't make dinner, my brothers will just eat Flamin' Hot Nacho Doritos."

Mrs. Singh's eyebrows furrowed again. "That sounds very unhealthy."

"Mom, it's okay if—" Didi started, but her mother cut her off.

"Indira, come help me pack up these samosas for Harriet's brothers," instructed Mrs. Singh. Although she was a tiny woman, it was clear she meant business. "You'll take them, won't you?" she asked Harriet.

"That would be delightful!" Harriet said.

"Good," said Mrs. Singh with a satisfied smile.

"Come, Indira." Turning toward the kitchen, Mrs. Singh shook her head and murmured, "Flamin' Hot Nacho Doritos?"

As Didi and her mom disappeared into the kitchen, Amelia looked at Harriet, eyebrows raised. "Enchanted?" asked Amelia. "Delightful?"

"What?" asked Harriet. "Parents love that stuff."

"Umm, royal parents maybe," said Amelia. "At Buckingham Palace."

"You're just jealous," teased Harriet, "because I got all the samosas."

"I come bearing gifts!" Harriet announced as she walked through her front door a half hour later. "A dozen vegetable samosas! And new logo sketches for the T-shirts!"

The boys crowded around the table and commenced a feeding frenzy. They fought over who got more samosas. Then they fought over the logos.

Didi had redrawn the animal in the first logo; now it looked less like a dinosaur and more like a lizard, which was as close as you could get to a recognizable skink. In the second logo option, she'd replaced the flowery script with jagged, angular letters. Way more rock and roll.

Didi had scrapped the Superman-style third option altogether, replacing it with a line drawing of a guitar with the band name written graffiti-style underneath. She'd added bright colors to each drawing, so they all popped. The girls had liked all three choices, and Resa had thought it a good idea to let the band choose. Easier said than done.

Joe voted for the guitar. Sam voted for the encircled band name, and Larry loved the skink.

"We gotta keep it real," Larry said, devouring a samosa. "Remember why we're doing this in the first place."

"That doesn't even make sense," Joe said, pushing his curtain of hair to the side. "And that was your fourth samosa. I had only three."

"Well, I can't give it back to you now," Larry replied. Turning to Harriet, he said, "Tell Didi thanks for the logos. They're really good. I'm calling it—she's the next Nico Fangelo."

"Who?" asked Joe.

"You know, the guy who painted that famous ceiling? In the church?" Larry looked annoyed at their lack of comprehension. "Seriously? Nobody knows who I'm . . . he's super famous!"

Larry wiped his hands on a napkin and walked

out of the room, shaking his head. "Some people have no culture."

Harriet watched him go, then helped herself to the last samosa.

"Nicofan—oh!" she exclaimed, a stroke of insight hitting her. "I got it! Michelangelo!"

~~~~~~

The next day at lunch, Harriet relayed Larry's message to Didi.

"Yeah, I think I've heard of Nico Fangelo," Didi said, laughing. "He was on the short list for the Sistine Chapel, I'm pretty sure." She sprinkled salt onto a hard-boiled egg.

"Your brothers are hilarious," said Resa, who'd finished eating. "My brother is just a pest."

Amelia took a long sip from her milk carton. "Ricky's a sweetheart."

"You say that because he hasn't tried to turn you into a persimmon yet," Resa replied. "Just you wait."

"But my brothers can't agree on a logo," said Harriet. "And I need to get Lucy the design today or there won't be enough time to make the T-shirts." She begrudgingly took a bite of her peanut-butter-and-jelly sandwich. She preferred peach jam to grape jelly, but when she'd told Joan that earlier, Joan had said, "I prefer a beach vacation to serving sandwiches."

"The problem with the band is there's too many cooks in that kitchen," said Resa. "Every group needs a leader for exactly this reason, to make executive decisions. Don't the Skinks have a leader?"

Harriet considered. "Joe's the front man and the lead singer."

Resa reached over to grab the pencil perpetually tucked behind Amelia's ear, then passed it and a napkin over to Harriet.

"Write Joe's number down, and I'll go text him in the lobby," said Resa. "I'll tell him to make a final decision."

Cell phone use was prohibited during the school day except for emergencies, and even then it was allowed only in the school lobby during lunch. Most students had a very liberal definition of what was an emergency, and so the lobby was often filled with kids dashing off quick messages during lunch. As long as you did it fast, before an old-school teacher like Ms. Davis passed by, it was usually fine.

"C'mon, Didi," said Resa, grabbing the napkin and standing. "You can be the lookout for Ms. Davis."

"Oh, goody," grumbled Didi, but she followed Resa out the double doors of the cafeteria.

Amelia took a bite of her turkey-and-cheese sandwich and chewed thoughtfully. "Hey, did you get the park permits for Friday? I don't want to get kicked out."

"Done!" Harriet sang. "Sam's best friend's dad's sister works for the parks department, and she's taking care of the permit."

"Well, if Sam's best friend's dad's sister's on it," said Amelia with a smile, "what could go wrong?"

"That's what I always say," replied Harriet.

"Don't forget I'm meeting you at dismissal to go to the high school," Amelia reminded Harriet while she crunched on a carrot stick. "We'll figure out the orders and sizes."

"I just hope we can untangle the mess I made," Harriet said, forcing herself to finish her sandwich, gross grape jelly and all.

"Oh, we will," said Amelia with confidence. "I am a master untangler. I should be bottled and used after shampooing."

Harriet laughed. "Good to know. But still, I'm sorry you have to spend all afternoon doing this."

"Please. You're doing me a favor, getting me out of tennis," said Amelia. "I can use a break from Resa kicking my butt."

"Yeah, I was surprised that you two are playing tennis together," said Harriet. "When we started working on the lemonade stand, you couldn't stand each other's guts."

Amelia shrugged. "Resa's bark is worse than her bite. She's really funny—and she's teaching me a lot about tennis. Though she can be a tad competitive."

Harriet laughed. "Just a tad."

As if on cue, Resa ran back into the cafeteria, earning a rebuke from Joan, who called after her, "You're gonna break your neck!" Didi trailed behind at a safe distance and normal speed.

"Well?" asked Harriet. "What's the verdict?"

"Option number two," said Resa, panting. "The circle. He thinks it's classic."

"Hey, Miss Lightspeed," called Joan from the food counter. "Can you pick up that tray you knocked over in your big rush?"

"I guess I'm not the only one living life in the fast lane," said Harriet.

Resa groaned as she headed back to deal with the tray mess. "You're also not the only one on Joan's bad side."

Amelia was right about being a master untangler. It took a while, but eventually she straightened out most of the orders—getting all the names down, along with the choice of adult unisex sizes. She apologized to Reginald and told him the most she could offer was a 25 percent discount. He changed his order and bought only one T-shirt, but as Amelia pointed out to Harriet, that was okay because they'd actually make more money than if he'd bought eight at half price.

"Math is an enigma," said Harriet, shaking her head.

Amelia laughed. "Math is anything but an enigma. That's why I like it. It's always the same. It's reliable."

They'd retreated to a bench near the high school's side entrance, where they were eating sourdough pretzel rods and going over the orders one last time to make sure they'd ironed out every wrinkle.

Amelia chomped thoughtfully on a pretzel. "What does this mean?" she asked, pointing to one of the order entries. "Here, next to Cam-Thu's order. It says three shirts in small, and then it says *LTR*. Is that supposed to be large?"

"Oh, that means 'later,'" Harriet explained. "She didn't have any money on her, so I told her to pay me whenever. Like a . . . whaddya call it . . . an IOU."

"Okay, see, the whole point of preorders is that there are no IOUs," said Amelia. "We need the cash to place the order. No money, no shirt. You read me?"

"I read you loud and clear! Roger that!" Harriet mimed speaking into a walkie-talkie. "Over and out!"

"Uh-huh," Amelia murmured uncertainly.

"Okay, okay," said Harriet with a sigh. "I'll go by Cam-Thu's house right now and collect."

Amelia closed the notebook and got to her feet. "I'll go with you. Then we can go to Lucy's shop to place the order."

wwwww

Cam-Thu was just getting home from debate practice when they arrived. As always, she was impeccably dressed in an outfit that could have appeared on the cover of a fashion magazine, from the bun she wore atop her head, with tiny tendrils hanging down, to the boots, which perfectly matched her belt.

Cam-Thu was two years older than Harriet and a role model in more ways than one. In particular, Harriet admired Cam-Thu's attention to detail; she was the master of the well-chosen accessory. Harriet wondered how long it took Cam-Thu to get dressed in the morning.

Not only did Cam-Thu fork over the money she owed Harriet, but she also gave Harriet a bag full of hand-me-downs, which included the world's skinniest tie, with pink and purple stripes.

"It matches your purple pleather jacket," said Cam-Thu.

"My power suit is complete!" exclaimed Harriet. She threw her arms around Cam-Thu's neck and squeezed. "Love you, Cam Cam."

"Watch the hair, Harry," Cam-Thu reminded her. "I've got a Skype study session in five, and I don't have time to battle with this hair doughnut."

Armed with a hefty wad of cash, the selected T-shirt logo, and a bag full of Cam-Thu hand-me-downs, the girls headed to Lucy's shop, a tiny storefront with a blue awning and SMALL JOYS written in gold script on the window.

It was an inviting little shop. The walls were painted a cheerful yellow, and pastel paper lanterns hung from the ceiling. Lovely things lined the shelves: small wooden jewelry boxes, embroidered pillows, silk headbands, corduroy stuffed animals, brightly colored bangles. Too bad there wasn't a customer in the store.

"Hel–lo, sweet pea!" Lucy sang when she caught sight of Harriet coming through the door. "Rambo! It's your best friend! Wake up, you sleepyhead!"

Lucy had a wide smile and big, bright eyes. She wore red reading glasses on a beaded chain around her neck and dangly silver earrings, which were easy to admire since her hair was shorn so short.

Everything about Lucy was round and soft, and when she walked over to give Harriet a hug, Harriet felt like a pillow was embracing her. It was nice. Harriet didn't really have grandparents—her mom's parents died when she was little and her dad's parents lived overseas. He didn't really talk to them, and Harriet couldn't remember the last time they'd visited. So she welcomed a grandmotherly hug from Lucy.

Harriet introduced Amelia to Lucy and told her they were ready to do business.

Lucy rubbed her hands together quickly. "Business time!" she called out. "I'll go get my order ledger.

Want to give Rambo a treat? You know where I keep 'em."

Lucy disappeared behind the blue velvet curtain leading to the back room, and Harriet reached over the counter, retrieving a cat treat from the lidded container there. "Here, Rambo," she called. A second later, an orange tabby cat who'd been dozing in the corner got to his feet and stretched lazily, then walked over to Harriet. Harriet let him eat the treat out of her palm, then scratched him between his ears.

"Isn't he the cutest?" she asked Amelia. "And isn't the store great?"

"Yeah," said Amelia. She added in a whisper, "Business is slow, huh?"

"Nobody even knows it's here," Harriet whispered back. "She's got great stuff, and it's not too expensive. But it's on this little side street, so nobody ever walks by."

Lucy pushed through the curtain, her reading glasses perched on the end of her nose and a thick black binder in her hands. She was frowning. "Harriet, sweet pea, I thought you were coming by yesterday with the money so that we could place an order." Her voice was apologetic. "My vendor needs six to eight business days for rush orders."

"We were a tad delayed," said Harriet, blushing. "But we have the money now. All of it. And the concert is one week from tomorrow, so we still have eight days."

"Yes, but that's only five business days," Lucy said. "Weekends don't count."

Rambo weaved in between Harriet's legs, purring. Harriet was too upset to notice, though. "Can't we try?" she asked plaintively. "Can't we rush the rush?"

"We can always try," said Lucy with a smile. "And with some luck, the order will get here next Friday." She pulled her glasses off and let them fall to her chest. "Of course, there's no telling what time of day they'll arrive. Might be in the evening—after your concert starts."

Harriet looked at Amelia nervously. She'd already messed things up so much. She didn't want to make the wrong call. "What should we do?"

Amelia drummed her fingers on the countertop. Then she said, "I say we go for it. Odds are in our favor, right?"

"Sure, sweet pea," said Lucy. "If you're a glass-is-half-full kind of person."

"Oh, we are," Harriet assured her. "We definitely are."

The week before the concert flew by. There was a ton of stuff to do—all sorts of little things Harriet hadn't anticipated.

The girls were so busy planning the concert that would raise money for Larry's new guitar that they kept forgetting to deal with one tiny but oh-so-important detail: Larry would need a guitar to play at that concert. And not just at the concert, he pointed out, but before, too. The Radical Skinks hadn't practiced in a while, and they couldn't just pick up and play a killer concert out of the blue.

The obvious thing to do, the girls agreed, was to

borrow a guitar for the week. Trouble was, while the boys knew plenty of guitarists, they were all using their instruments to practice for the Battle of the Bands.

Thankfully, Harriet possessed superpowers of persuasion. She paid a visit to Music Mania, the music store on Pecan Street, and struck up a conversation with the owner, a heavily tattooed woman named Mo. Harriet told Mo the sad story of how she'd accidentally destroyed Larry's guitar—and possibly his dreams of stardom—and how she was doing everything she could to make things right. "The one thing we still desperately need," she said, her eyes wide and hopeful, "is to borrow a guitar for Larry to practice with this week. Can you help?"

Mo hooked her fingers into the belt loops of her jeans. "What's in it for me?"

"How about some free publicity?" asked Harriet with a smile. "We'll put a stack of Music Mania brochures on the merch table!"

"Nah," said Mo without hesitation. "Nobody takes brochures. What else you got?"

"Ummmm . . ." Harriet was surprised. Usually her soft sell did the trick, but Mo clearly required a hard sell. "We can hang a poster up behind the merch table."

"I want ten shout-outs on social media from the lead singer's account," said Mo.

"Okay," Harriet agreed.

"I'm not done." Mo went on. Her face barely moved when she talked. She looked like a ventriloquist, just without the dummy. "I also want a shout-out at the opening of the concert. Including our address."

"That's a lot of conditions," said Harriet. She couldn't help but admire Mo's negotiation skills.

"And," said Mo.

"There's more?" asked Harriet.

"I need a guarantee that your brother will buy his guitar here when he raises the money," said Mo. She extended her hand toward Harriet. "Do we have a deal?"

"You drive a hard bargain," said Harriet, pausing a moment. Then she reached out and shook Mo's hand firmly. "Nice doing business with you."

Larry was delighted to get his hands on a guitar again—especially the ChromaChord 3000.

"This guitar's way better than Herbert, may he rest in peace," Larry said. "It plays like a dream. I mean, with this ax, I could be Keith Richards."

"You should get that kind, then, when we raise the money," said Amelia. She'd come over for an organizational meeting about the concert.

"You think we'll have enough money?" Larry asked.

"Depends. How much did Mo say this one cost, Harriet?"

"One hundred and forty," said Harriet. "I bet she gave us a more expensive one on purpose! She knew Larry would fall in love with it."

"She's one smart cookie, that Mo," said Amelia admiringly. "She must teach us her ways."

"All I know is, I need this guitar," said Larry. "With this baby, I could be Hendrix!"

"Hendrix?" whispered Amelia to Harriet. "Now he's going too far."

~~~~~~

Thanks to the new ChromaChord 3000, Larry's solos soared. The boys rehearsed every night for hours on end. Their long break from rehearsals had made them sloppy, and they had a lot of work to do before the Battle of the Bands.

The Radical Skinks' work ethic was admirable—but it was also very loud. Harriet's dad owned a pair of noise-canceling headphones, which he usually only wore when he worked on a painting or sculpture and needed to be free of distractions. These headphones became a hot commodity in the Nguyen household.

"Harriet, you've had the headphones for over an hour," complained her dad on Thursday night. The boys had been practicing for two hours straight and showed no signs of stopping soon.

"What?" she asked. Sam was whaling on his drum kit, and she couldn't hear a thing.

"You're hogging the headphones! I need them!" her dad shouted.

"Oh no you don't!" broke in Harriet's mom. *"I need those for my customer downstairs!"*

"For your custard? You're baking?" Harriet's dad yelled.

The house, always loud, became deafening.

But every night, the band sounded better—tighter and more in sync. They sounded like American Supahstars.

Harriet popped into Small Joys every afternoon on her way home from school to see if there was any update on the T-shirt order. Every afternoon, Lucy told her the same thing: It would be Friday at the earliest.

"The concert's Friday night," Harriet lamented to Lucy.

"I know, sweet pea," Lucy replied. "I've got my fingers crossed."

On Friday at lunch, Harriet led the girls into the school's lobby and borrowed Resa's phone to call Small Joys.

"Are they in yet?" she asked anxiously.

"Well, hello to you, too, Harriet," Lucy teased. "A bunch of boxes were just delivered. I'll have to go through and see if your order's in one of them."

"Do you think that will take more than eight minutes?" asked Harriet. "Because that's how much longer we have for lunch, and then we have to turn the phone off and I won't be able to concentrate on my prealgebra quiz and if I don't concentrate, I will for sure fail—"

"Okay, okay," Lucy interrupted. "I'm opening the boxes now. I'll call you back in a minute."

The girls huddled around Resa's phone, keeping an eye out for Ms. Davis.

"We have only five minutes left," Didi said, yanking her sleeves down so she didn't succumb to temptation and bite her nails. "What's taking so long?"

"Whatcha waiting for?" came a high-pitched voice from behind Harriet.

Harriet spun around to find their classmate Val peeking into their little cluster.

"Nosy much?" asked Resa, her whole body tensing up. Val and Resa always seemed to be in competition. Whether it was for the best grades or to win a lemonade-selling contest, they both were intent on coming out on top. Resa didn't know why Val was poking her head in their business, but it didn't bode well.

"I'm just a concerned citizen," said Val, looking mock-offended. "Phones are for emergencies only, so I figured it must be an emergency." She smiled, and her braces glinted in the light. But that was nothing compared with the glint of the silver-sequined emoji on her shirt.

"Just making sure we have our T-shirts for the big concert tonight," explained Harriet. "You're coming, right?"

"Wouldn't miss it," said Val. "You didn't forget to put in my order, did you?"

Resa fixed Val with a skeptical look. "You're getting a T-shirt? You know they don't have sequins on them, right?"

Val pursed her lips together, obviously annoyed. "I don't need sequins on my Radical Skinks T-shirt," she said with a sugary, sweet smile. "Mine is special enough without any bling." She winked at Harriet, then turned on her heel. "See you tonight."

As soon as she was out of earshot, Resa turned to Harriet. "What was that wink for?"

"We're friends!" Harriet protested. "It was just a friendly wink!"

Resa crossed her arms over her chest. "Uh-huh."

"Do you two have an arrangement for something special?" asked Amelia. "On the T-shirt?"

Harriet had the feeling she'd done something wrong, but she couldn't figure out what. This was a common feeling for Harriet, and it unsettled her. "I mean, maybe she's talking about the autographs?" Harriet said. "She wanted all my brothers to sign her shirt. Who would've guessed she's such a fan, right?"

"You charged her more, right?" asked Resa.

Ah, so that's what my mistake was, Harriet thought. Still, she didn't get it. "Why would I?" she asked nervously. "I mean, it's not a big deal. My brothers love giving autographs. They don't mind. Really."

The lobby started filling up with students leaving the lunchroom and heading to their next class. The bell hadn't rung yet, but Harriet knew it would any second.

"This is why you need to run stuff by—" Resa began, but Didi elbowed her.

"It's *not* a big deal," said Didi. "But next time, you should charge more for an autographed shirt."

"But it doesn't cost us any more to get the autographs!" Harriet protested.

"That's true," Amelia said. "But now everyone else's shirts—that they're buying for the same price—will be less special by comparison. It's like—"

Amelia's voice was interrupted by the bell blaring.

"Doggonit!" Harriet exclaimed. "Lucy said she'd call us back."

"I have to go to social studies," said Amelia. "Can't keep ancient Egypt waiting."

Resa placed her finger on the phone's off switch, but before she could press it down, it started to buzz. A text had just come in.

"It's from Lucy," Resa announced. "The shirts are in!"

The girls let out a celebratory whoop, just as Ms. Davis passed by. She glanced down at the phone in Resa's hand with disdain.

"Somebody break a bone?" she said.

"Uh, no," stammered Didi, looking mortified. "Sorry, Ms. Davis . . . we were—"

Ms. Davis held her hand up. "Save the song and dance for theater class," she said. "Which you're late for, if I'm not mistaken."

Didi's eyes were wide and worried. "Ohmigosh, yes, yes, you're right, I'm—I'm going."

Didi, Resa, and Amelia scattered to various staircases to make it to their next period on time. Harriet took a step toward the stairs and then had a thought. She spun around and called out, "Hey, Ms. D, do you like rock and roll?"

"Skinks tees! Come get your commemorative Skinks tees here!"

Harriet stood behind the merchandise table at the entrance to the park, an orange megaphone pressed to her mouth. Her voice was near deafening through the megaphone.

"Step right up! Step right up!" she went on. "Get your super-stylish Radical Skinks stuff!"

Amelia stood next to Harriet, folding T-shirts into piles. She winced. "Harriet, can you maybe lower the volume? Just a bit?"

Harriet looked at her with a bright smile. "That

would defeat the whole purpose, silly! Gotta be heard, right?" She turned to face the group just entering the park. "Teeeeeeee-shirts!" she bellowed. "While supplies last!"

Harriet gestured with a flourish at the T-shirt she was sporting, a bona fide Skinks tee. No one would ever have guessed from her 100-watt smile and chirpy voice that she thought the shirt was absolutely hideous.

Okay, *hideous* was the wrong word. The T-shirt was too boring to even be hideous.

Drab. That's what it was. Dreary. Bleeeeeeegh.

If someone had tried to give her one of these T-shirts for free, she'd say, "Thanks, but no thanks." No way would she ever be caught wearing the epic fashion fail that was this T-shirt. And yet, here she was, not only asking people to wear the T-shirts, but asking them to pay twenty-five dollars for the privilege. Thank merciful heavens she was a great actress.

After some more shouting, Harriet put the megaphone down on the merch table and turned to Amelia. "We should've gone with the cherry-red shirt. Or lime green! Or yellow! Something eye-catching. Anything but . . ." She made a disgusted face. "White."

"White is the perfect color for a T-shirt!" Amelia replied. In fact, basic colors—white, black, and especially gray—were her favorites. Her closet was dominated by shades of gray—from slate to platinum to moon glow. "You can't go wrong with a basic color. It matches with everything!"

"Yeah, it matches really well with this ink," Resa chimed in. "So well I can't even see the writing." Resa looked down disdainfully at her own T-shirt, the same bona fide Radical Skinks tee. "Why'd you go with light gray ink, Harriet? Were they out of invisible ink?"

"Ha. Ha. Ha," Harriet grumbled gloomily. "Very funny. I was going for a minimalist look! It's very in right now! And I was in a rush to place the order, if you'll recall! We didn't have time for a sample!"

"Well, it's too late now," Didi broke in sensibly. "We have to act like these T-shirts are high fashion."

Harriet lifted the megaphone to her mouth. "Ooooooh-ooh! Style *and* comfort? These shirts have it alllllll!"

"Just like that!" said Didi. "You deserve an Oscar."

"Thanks," said Harriet, but without her usual pep.

At least the weather was good, Harriet reasoned. She'd been worried about rain all week, but the afternoon had turned out to be gorgeous—not a cloud in the sky. Not too hot and not too cold; perfect T-shirt weather. If only the T-shirts were not so grim and bleak.

Didi elbowed Harriet to rouse her from her day-dream. "We've got a customer!"

"Hell-o!" Harriet sang, beaming at the small, dark-haired girl in front of her. She had three piercings in her left earlobe and a hoop in her lip. Harriet wanted to ask if they hurt but thought better of it.

"I ordered a T-shirt," the girl said. "Dondelstein."

Harriet scanned the order sheet, which Amelia had typed up, printed, and attached to a clipboard. She couldn't find the name. "Uhh, okay . . . Is Dondelstein your first or last name?" she asked.

The girl fixed her with a withering stare for a long moment. Finally, she said through gritted teeth, "Last."

"Hello!" sang Didi with high-octane enthusiasm, taking the clipboard from Harriet's hands. "Let's just take a quick little look here." She scanned the list, once, then twice. "Uh-huh . . . hmmm . . . one moment, please!"

She turned her back on the customer and beckoned the other girls over.

"Her name's not on here," whispered Didi.

"I know," Harriet whispered back.

"Do you recognize her from when you collected money at the high school?" Resa whispered.

Harriet shook her head. "And I'm sure I didn't sell to her. I never forget a face."

Resa spun around toward the girl.

"Are you sure you preordered?" she asked.

"Uhhhh, yeah," the girl replied. "Because I'm not an idiot."

Resa's eyes narrowed in anger. "Well, your name's not on here. So I don't know what to tell you."

Amelia stepped in. "Do you remember what day you met Harriet after school?"

"I didn't meet her," the girl said with a scowl. "I don't know who this girl is."

"Then who'd you give your money to?" asked Resa impatiently.

The girl rolled her eyes dramatically. "Joe," she said. "In Spanish class."

"Joe took your money? Perfect! As if this mess isn't complicated enough—" Resa started in what was obviously going to be a rant. Didi, sensing this, yanked on her elbow and pulled her away.

"Just one more little moment, ma'am," Didi said.

"Ma'am?" the girl scoffed. "You have got to be kidding me."

Didi joined the huddle that Resa, Harriet, and Amelia had formed behind the table.

"Did you know Joe was collecting money?" Resa asked Harriet. "That makes everything way more complicated! Did he write his orders down? Where's the money for his orders?"

Harriet shrugged, panic in her eyes.

"Let's go ask him," suggested Amelia.

"Oh, no no no!" Harriet's eyebrows wrinkled up. "Joe doesn't like to be disturbed before a show. He's in the zone, and he has to be left alone. Otherwise, the show'll be ruined. It jinxes him!"

Amelia smirked. "That's ridiculous."

"No, it's true!" Harriet insisted. "Every time I've bothered him when he was in the zone, the show was a mess!"

"Uhh, sorry to interrupt your little meeting or whatever, but any chance you could give me the T-shirt I paid for?" the Dondelstein girl asked.

"What do we do about Snarky Snarkerson over here?" asked Amelia.

"We should give her a T-shirt," said Didi with assurance.

"Are we operating on the honor system now?" asked Resa.

"Annnnny day now would be fine," said the girl.

Resa spun around, grabbed the first T-shirt her hand clutched, and tossed it at the girl. "Here. Next!"

"That's not even my size—"

"Take it up with customer service!" snapped Resa.

The Dondelstein girl shook her head. "You people are the worst," she muttered as she walked away.

"*Us?*" Resa sputtered, flabbergasted. "*We're* the worst?!"

Didi laid a hand on Resa's arm, ready to offer

some reassurance, but her words were drowned out by the high-pitched squeals emanating from Harriet's mouth. Equally high-pitched squeals were coming from Cam-Thu, who stood on the other side of the merch table. The cousins hugged awkwardly over the table, still squealing.

"Sooooooo," said Cam-Thu when she let go of Harriet, "where are these T-shirts I've been hearing so much about? I must see them!"

Harriet flung her arms to the side and spun around. "Ta-da!"

Cam-Thu wrinkled the top of her nose like she'd smelled something rancid. "Nooooooo," she said, waving her hand as if to shoo away the offensive odor. "No no no no no."

"It's *understated*," Harriet said.

"Harry," said Cam-Thu, tilting her head to the side and narrowing her eyes, "you *know* I don't do white. Or crewneck tees. Where are the V-necks? And tanks? Where are the colors?"

"White is a color," Amelia argued. She knew it was nothing personal, but she felt defensive.

"It doesn't matter," said Cam-Thu decisively. "I'll just take my money back."

"Umm, okay." Harriet looked stressed. "Just hold on—"

"We can't," Amelia jumped in. "We used the money to pay for the T-shirts. They're nonrefundable."

"I'm not wearing that T-shirt," exclaimed Cam-Thu. "It's worse than those weird gowns they give you in the hospital!"

"Lemme talk to my associates, Cam Cam," Harriet said with a smile. "Come back after the show."

"Fine," said Cam-Thu. She leaned over to Harriet and whispered, "They can't force you to wear that, you know. It's a free country."

Amelia'd had about enough of Cam-Thu and her fashion advice. She waved over the next person in line. "Next!"

The next half hour whizzed by as the girls tried to distribute preordered T-shirts. The hardest part was getting people to accept the shirts once they saw them. Lots of people asked for a refund.

"Who are the Radical Skunks?" asked one teenager with red curly hair.

"It's not 'skunks'!" Harriet protested. "It's 'skinks.'"

"Yeah, of course it is" said the redhead. "So why do your T-shirts say 'The Radical Skunks'?"

Harriet scrutinized a shirt, bringing it close to her face and then pulling it away for a better look. The logo had been perfectly readable when she gave it to Lucy, but it had printed out way smaller than she'd expected—and now the word *skinks* was sort of squashed. The boy was right—the *i* did look a little like a *u*.

"'Cause the thing is, I hate skunks," the redhead reflected. "I was at sleepaway camp this one time, and we were on a hike, and I went out in the woods to use the bathroom, you know? So I ran into this skunk. And I musta scared him, because he let loose on me, right? And ever since then, everyone at camp called me Skunky. That was five years ago." He shook his head decisively. "I cannot wear this T-shirt. I need a refund."

Harriet knew Amelia didn't want to issue refunds, but she couldn't help but feel sorry for this guy. I mean, did she want to be responsible for kids calling him Skunky even just one more time? She pulled a crumpled twenty and five singles out of her wallet—her saved-up allowance money. She glanced to her left, then her right, to make sure no one was looking. "Here," said Harriet, handing him the cash quickly. "Just keep it hush-hush. We don't want word getting out that we're doing refunds."

"Hush money," said the redhead, nodding. "Got it."

But a few minutes later, a cluster of three girls walked up to the table demanding a refund from Amelia and Didi.

"Sorry," said Amelia, shrugging. "The shirts are nonrefundable."

The tallest one, with hair pulled back into two tight braids, pursed her lips. "Then why'd you give a refund to Jeremiah?"

"Who is Jeremiah?" asked Didi.

"Oh," said the shortest friend, who wore blue lipstick and blue nail polish. "You probably know him as Skunky."

Harriet overheard the exchange from where she was crouching a few feet away, drawing chalk arrows on the sidewalk by the park entrance to direct people to the concert. She felt the need to intervene and rushed over, chalky-fingered. "See, that was a one-time thing," she explained. "Because of his emotional pain and suffering."

"Harriet!" Amelia scolded her.

The third girl in the cluster, whose eyebrows had been plucked into a thin, high arch, blinked one time slowly. It was a "Listen up, 'cause I won't say this twice" sort of blink. "I don't fry jalapeño poppers all weekend at the Burger Barn so I can throw my money away on lousy T-shirts with typos on them."

"It says 'skinks'!" Didi protested. "The *i* just printed out kind of squashed."

The girl with the arched eyebrows blinked again slowly.

So Amelia, Resa, and Didi pooled the money

they'd brought from home to go out for a celebratory dinner and gave all three girls refunds.

"We are hemorrhaging money," Amelia moaned to Harriet and Resa as Didi helped the next customer. "We haven't sold even one extra shirt tonight, and we've had to give refunds on four."

"Hey," Didi interrupted, "where's the rest of the large shirts? I can't find them."

"We're out," Resa said. "I just handed off the last one."

Didi scanned the order sheet, making marks next to several names with her pencil. "But we have four more larges on this list who still haven't picked up their order. I don't understand. Most of these crossed-out orders are for smalls and mediums. What happened to all the large shirts?"

Harriet peered over Didi's shoulder at the order sheet. "Oh, I had to give some of those people large shirts instead of mediums. These shirts run really small!"

Didi pushed her glasses up the bridge of her nose. "But what are we going to give to this guy? He paid for a large, and that's what he wants." She nodded at the customer waiting at the table. The right side of his face was painted blue, and he had a streak of blue running through the middle of his brown Mohawk.

"It's Reginald!" exclaimed Harriet. "He's the one

who originally bought eight shirts when he thought they were half price. He *needs* a large T-shirt!"

"Yes, okay, we agree," said Resa. "But where do we get it from?"

Harriet squeezed her eyes shut and hummed.

"What's she doing?" whispered Didi.

"I think she's thinking," said Amelia.

Harriet's eyes flew open, and she spun to face Amelia. She grabbed the large Radical Skinks tee Amelia wore, which she'd tied at the waist.

"Gimme!" Harriet cried.

"Ah!" screeched Amelia. "I'm under attack!"

"Your shirt!" Harriet cried. "It's a large! Hand it over!"

"Ew! No!" protested Amelia, squirming away from her.

"Wait, she's right," said Resa. "You're wearing a tank top underneath, right?"

"Yeah, sure, but . . ." Amelia started. "I'm *wearing* this! You're literally asking me for the shirt off my back."

"Yep," said Resa.

"Hand it over," said Harriet.

"Excuse me?" called Reginald. "Did you find my shirt? The show's gonna start any minute."

Harriet rushed out from behind the table and positioned herself slightly behind Reginald so that he'd have to turn his back on the merch table to talk to her. "Reggie!" she said. "You made it!"

"Uh, it's Reginald," he said. "So what's the deal with my shirt?"

While Harriet distracted Reginald, Amelia untied the knot in her T-shirt, slipped it off, and handed it to Resa, who shook it out furiously, trying to smooth the wrinkles.

Didi grabbed the green apple body mist she always kept in her backpack and spritzed it a few times on the T-shirt, hoping it would make it seem fresh and new. The smell was so strong that Resa and Didi instantly started coughing and gagging.

"Ugh! It smells like we dunked it in a bucket of apple juice," lamented Resa.

"Seriously, I want my shirt," Reginald was saying. He was visibly annoyed, losing patience.

"*Your shirt is coming right up!*" shouted Harriet to Reginald in an attempt to hurry things along.

"Just hold your horses, would you?" snapped Amelia, smoothing down her dark gray tank top.

"Yeah, we've got your shirt right here," Resa said, tossing it at him.

Reginald caught the shirt and grimaced.

"Why does it smell like this?" he said, pinching his nose with his free hand.

"It's *apples!*" barked Resa. "Who doesn't like apples?"

"I want another one," Reginald insisted. "One that smells normal. And isn't all wrinkly."

"Listen, guy," said Resa, who had depleted all her stores of patience and flexibility, "this is all we've got. Take it or leave it."

"It's like they say in kindergarten," added Didi. "You get what you get, and you don't get upset."

Reginald said nothing for a moment, then he raised his eyebrows and shook his head slowly. "The Radical Skinks deserve better than you all," he said as he turned to walk away.

Harriet flushed with anger. How dare he?

"You've got it all wrong!" she found herself shouting at top volume. "The Radical Skinks deserve better than *you!*"

As the girls watched Reginald recede, a silence fell over the group.

"So, that was bad," observed Resa.

"That's putting it mildly," said Amelia.

"When is this show going to start anyway?" asked Didi, near tears. "I just want this to be over already."

"Harriet, can you please go check on your brothers?" asked Resa. "They're fifteen minutes late, and they've got to start before anyone else asks for more refunds."

"All right," said Harriet begrudgingly. "But if I jinx them, it's on you."

"We'll take that risk," said Amelia as she donned a too-tight size small Radical Skinks tee. "Go, go, go!"

Harriet slipped out from behind the merch table and raced toward the backstage area, which was really just a bench between two oak trees. Halfway there, she collided with an obstacle. A very sparkly obstacle.

"Sorry, Val!" Harriet exclaimed, scrambling to her feet. "I gotta run—"

"Wait!" Val grabbed her arm. "Are you going to see the band?"

"Uh, yeah, actually—"

"Perfect!" Val pressed a Radical Skinks T-shirt into Harriet's hands. "Don't forget to make them sign this! Make sure you get all three signatures. And be sure to use this gold marker." She handed a metallic Sharpie to Harriet. "It'll look best on the white shirt."

"You brought your own gold marker?" asked Harriet, her voice a mix of disbelief and admiration. "How'd you know what color the shirt would be?"

"I didn't," said Val with a shrug. "I brought an entire Sharpie collection." She patted her backpack. "You can never be too prepared."

Unless you're the Startup Squad, thought Harriet.

Harriet found her brothers collected around the park bench and decked out in concert garb, which consisted of denim for Larry, fake leather for Joe, and huge amounts of hair gel for Sam.

Joe sat cross-legged on one end of the bench, his eyes closed and his hands palms up in a meditative pose. Sam sat next to him, swiping at his phone. Larry knelt on the ground, frowning and fiddling with an amp.

"Hi, guys!" Harriet chirped.

Joe snapped his eyes open and glared at her. "Harry! What are you doing? You know I'm in the zone!"

"I know. I just wanted to see how it's going," Harriet said. "And see if I could get you guys to sign this—"

"So *stupid!*" yelled Larry, standing and giving the amp a kick.

"I'm sorry!" said Harriet. "But you don't have to be mean—"

"Not you," Larry said. "The amp. It keeps glitching, turning on and off."

Sam glanced up from his phone for a second. "Did you try unplugging—"

"Of *course* I tried unplugging it!" Larry interrupted.

"What about jiggling the—" Sam said.

"Sam! I tried jiggling the thing!" Larry was fully exasperated. "It's fried! The stupid thing's more fried than a drumstick at Nantucket Fried Chicken!"

"You mean Kentu—" Harriet started.

"Everyone," Joe scolded, eyes squeezed tight. "Respect the zone!"

"Well, there's nothing we can do about the amp now," said Sam in a whisper. He touched the top of his hair gently to make sure it was still shellacked into place. "We don't have another one."

Larry sighed loudly. "I'll go set this up on stage. But I wanna go on record that this is going to be a disaster."

"It's on the official record," said Sam.

Harried jumped in front of Larry and shoved the T-shirt and gold marker into his hand.

"Before you go, sign this super fast, would you?" she asked. "Use my back." She spun around and flattened her back into a suitable writing surface.

Larry sighed again, even louder this time, but he dutifully signed, then handed the marker to Sam, who did the same without even taking his eyes off his phone.

"Give Joe the marker," Harriet told Sam.

"He's in the zone," Sam warned.

"He's in zone overtime!" Harriet replied. "The show was supposed to start twenty minutes ago."

Sam pressed the marker into Joe's open palm. "Harry says you gotta sign the shirt."

Joe opened one eye, then the other. He looked accusingly at Harriet, who, still in flattened-back position, shuffled over to the bench so that Joe didn't have to move.

"Remember our show at the Salt Factory?" he asked Harriet. "Last spring?"

"Yeah," Harriet replied. "But, Joe, that was because you had a sore throat. It would've happened no matter what."

"It was because I was in the *zone* and I got *interrupted*!" Joe snapped. "So I got jinxed, and I sounded like Kermit the Frog. And let me remind you that I did not choose those words—the reviewer did when she blogged about it."

"I know—" Harriet said.

"Kermit the Frog," Joe repeated, uncapping the marker. "Those were her exact words."

He leaned over and signed his name hurriedly on the bottom of the T-shirt, then handed the shirt and the marker to Harriet, who stood and stretched her back out.

"My zone has been completely broken now, Harry," said Joe, and his voice was somber. "There's no stopping the jinx now. I only hope I don't get struck by lightning."

"Sorry, bro!" called Harriet over her shoulder as she ran out of the backstage area. "Good luck!"

Harriet found Val standing next to the merch table, making unhelpful observations that were clearly driving Resa to the brink of her sanity.

"What you need is a system," said Val.

"I've been saying the same thing," muttered Didi, not as quietly as she'd intended.

"We *have* a system!" Resa shot back at Val.

"You call that big old heap of shirts a system?" asked Val, her eyebrows raised.

"Yes!" Resa spun around to face Val so suddenly that her arm accidentally hit an open bottle of lemonade that Amelia had set down on the table. It fell over, directly on top of the shirts, and was half empty by the time Resa had the presence of mind to grab it.

"No. Way." Amelia lifted a T-shirt from the pile to check out the damage. There was a huge wet splotch on the side, and a stream of lemonade trickled down onto the table.

"This is my point exactly," said Val, putting her hands on her hips.

Resa turned to face Val again, this time with excruciating slowness.

"If you're not out of my face in five seconds . . ." growled Resa.

She didn't need to finish her thought. Val beat a hasty retreat, though not before grabbing her marker and signed T-shirt out of Harriet's hands.

"*Why* would you leave a bottle full of lemonade right next to our product?" asked Resa.

"Oh no, you don't." Amelia shook her head firmly. "This is all on you."

"Please!" Didi pleaded. "Let's just clean up the mess!"

"*Hello, Market Street!*" boomed Joe's voice. Harriet breathed a sigh of relief. The concert was starting. The crowd, too, seemed relieved. They let out a roar of appreciation.

"*Are we ready to—*"

Suddenly Joe's booming voice dropped out. A

second later, it boomed back, midsentence. *"—arty started!"*

There was some scattered applause, but the crowd seemed confused. So were the girls at the merch table.

"What's up with the sound system?" asked Amelia as she wrung out a drenched T-shirt.

"They're just having some amp problems," Harriet said. "No big deal."

She heard Sam hit his drumsticks together and count off: "A five! Six! . . ."

In the silence that followed, someone in the crowd yelled, "Did you forget how to count, dude?"

"Oh no," Harriet moaned. "Joe was right! It's the jinx!"

14

"There's no such thing," said Amelia confidently, "as a jinx."

"There is," insisted Harriet. "And this was a whopper of a jinx. This was the jinx to end all jinxes."

The concert had just ended, and the girls were cleaning up their table, sorting the soaked shirts from the not-soaked ones and packing leftover supplies in boxes. A few customers hadn't picked up their T-shirts yet. And the girls were hoping they'd just forget all about the shirts, because most of the ones they had left were super citrusy, and not in a good way.

"I'm with Amelia," said Resa. "The problem was a broken amp, not a curse."

"It wasn't just a broken amp, though," Didi observed quietly. "What about the drum?"

"Sam just hit it a little too hard," said Resa. "And poked a little hole in the top."

"He's been playing the drums since he was six," said Harriet, "and that has never happened. He once broke a drumstick because he hit the drums so hard, but he's never broken a drum."

"No matter what it was," said Amelia, "the crowd did not like it. They did not like it at all."

Didi grimaced. "Yeah, when they started chanting 'Rad Skinks stink'? That was pretty ugly."

Harriet dropped her head into her hands. "It's all my fault! I broke Joe's zone!"

"You!" The voice cut through Harriet's gloom, snapping her back to attention. Reginald was standing in front of her, his finger pointed straight at her face. He was not happy. "You broke Joe's zone! I saw you! This is all your fault!"

"Nobody asked you," Resa replied without missing a beat.

Reginald looked different, and it took Harriet a few seconds to figure out why. He was now wearing a Radical Skinks T-shirt. But it wasn't the one he'd bought, at least Harriet didn't think so, because it had her brothers' three signatures on it, in the exact locations where they'd signed before the concert started.

"Where—" Harriet said, totally confused. "Where'd you get that T-shirt?"

"Why should I tell you anything?" Reginald replied.

"Come on, Reg!" Harriet coaxed. "I'm sorry I insulted you. I was just delirious from the apple fumes."

"Yeah, that smell was revolting," said Reginald. He scanned the crowd exiting the park. "I got the shirt from that girl over there."

There was a glint as Val's sequined shirt caught the light of the setting sun.

"That girl just gave you her shirt?" asked Resa, incredulously.

"Sure, after I gave her fifty bucks," Reginald said. "She set it all up with me days ago."

As Reginald walked away, Resa looked at Harriet, her eyes wide and emphatic. "Told you."

"At least someone's making money off our T-shirts," Harriet muttered.

Joe, Sam, and Larry, looking haggard, approached the merch table.

"What was that about?" asked Joe. "He did not seem like a happy customer."

"There were some problems with the T-shirts," replied Resa.

"Well, there were some problems with our performance, so at least we're consistent," said Sam. His pompadour had collapsed, and bits of hair were going in every direction.

"Not only don't we have enough money to get a guitar, we now have to replace a drum," said Larry. "Which is even more expensive than a guitar. There is no way we can play at the Battle of the Bands now."

"Thanks a lot, Harriet," said Joe, his voice dripping with sarcasm. "Thanks for everything."

Harriet lay in bed. She wasn't sleeping but had
decided to pretend she was.

"Harriiiiiiet!" came her mother's voice, again,
from downstairs. "Come dooooooooown!"

No, Harriet decided. She would not come down
to breakfast—or, more likely, lunch, since it was two
o'clock in the afternoon. She was too demoralized,
too defeated, too glum, to talk to her mother. So she
stayed put, lying under the covers, with Zappa on her
belly.

"Haaaaaaaarry!" her mother yelled.

Harriet was hiding from her brothers—all of

them, even Larry—because they all hated her. She couldn't blame them. After all, she'd jinxed them and turned their show into a train wreck. The only place in the house where she definitely wouldn't run into them was her room. So there she would stay, forever if necessary.

Harriet's stomach growled. She hadn't eaten anything all day, and her stomach was running out of patience.

There was a knock on her bedroom door. Harriet squeezed her eyes shut and slid down farther under the covers.

She heard the door creak open and several sets of footsteps. Was it her mother or her brothers coming to confront her about how she'd messed everything up?

"Now this is what I call sleeping in," came Resa's voice.

Harriet opened her eyes to see Resa and Amelia standing by her bed. Didi, her long hair jammed under a baseball cap, hovered by the door like she was prepared to bolt at any moment.

Harriet looked at the girls for a minute, trying to decide her next move. Then she yanked the covers over her head.

"Harriet." Amelia giggled as she peeled the covers back down.

"We've been calling you all morning," said Didi

from the door. "Your mom kept saying you were sleeping."

"Finally, we had to come and make sure you were still alive," Amelia said.

"Well, I am," said Harriet. She stroked Zappa on her stomach. "I'm just dandy."

"What's the matter, Harry?" asked Didi, her brown eyes full of concern behind her glasses. She took a few tentative steps closer to the bed. "Why are you pulling a Rip Van Winkle?"

Harriet busied herself, picking a loose thread on the wrist of her pajamas. "My brothers hate me," she said quietly. "For real this time."

"No, they don't!" Didi protested.

"They're just mad. Big deal," said Resa, pulling up Harriet's desk chair. "My brother's mad at me, like, ninety percent of the time."

"But they're all mad at me. And the worst part is, I deserve it," said Harriet. She swallowed hard to make the lump in her throat go away. "I broke Larry's guitar, and it's my fault Sam's drum is busted. I ruined the T-shirts. Then I jinxed the band. I ruined everything."

"Nuh-uh," said Resa, clapping her hands together quickly to shake Harriet out of her sadness. "Sit up, Harriet Nguyen."

Without even meaning to, Harriet followed Resa's

instructions. Zappa, roused by the movement, slithered into Harriet's pajama sleeve to hide.

"Pity party's over," said Resa. Her voice was so firm that it took Harriet a minute to realize Resa was cheering her up. "You did not break Sam's drum. He broke it all by himself. You did not ruin the T-shirts. We all made those T-shirts together." She paused for a second, then said quickly, "You did break Larry's guitar, and that is totally on you, but so what? Everybody makes mistakes."

Harriet was surprised to find she felt considerably more cheerful. "You really don't think it's my fault?"

"I already said so once," said Resa. She grabbed Harriet's hand and pulled her to her feet. "Now get dressed."

Harriet placed Zappa gently on her bed and pulled the covers up over her green scaly body. "She needs her beauty rest," she said, walking to her closet. "So where are we going, anyway?"

"For ice cream!" sang Didi, inching toward the door. Now that Zappa was loose, she was ready to hit the road.

"I do love ice cream," said Harriet. "It always turns the glum into fun."

"It does," said Amelia. "And it gets the brain fired up, too."

A half hour later, the girls walked through the door of the ice-cream shop near the park. The bell on the door jangled, and Eleanor looked up from the stool where she sat behind the counter, a calculus textbook open on her lap. She closed the book and got to her feet.

"Twenty minutes!" Resa grumbled. "I *still* can't believe it."

"These outfits won't pick themselves," said Harriet, gesturing to her yellow tunic covered in enormous black peonies, which perfectly matched the large yellow flower clipped onto her side ponytail.

"How long does it take *you* to get dressed, Resa?" asked Amelia.

"Exactly two and a half minutes," replied Resa with pride. "Three if you count tying my Converse."

"Speaking of clothes," Harriet said to Eleanor, "I love your dress. Are those . . . pockets?"

Eleanor was in a white button-down shirt with short sleeves under a burgundy corduroy dress, with black combat boots. Eleanor always wore outfits whose components seemed totally incompatible but somehow came together just right on her. Now she slid her hands into the dress pockets and struck a pose like a fashion model. "Oh, I *gotta* have pockets," she said.

She stepped over to the counter and pulled an ice-cream scooper out of a cylinder full of cold water. "What can I get you, ladies?"

"Strawberry in a cup," Resa said without hesitation.

"Nice going, Pistachio." Eleanor smiled. "A girl who knows what she wants!"

Harriet was confused. "Didn't you just say strawberry?"

Resa smiled. "It's her nickname for me. Because the first time I came in, I couldn't make a decision to save my life—until I decided I wanted pistachio."

Eleanor was a whiz with a scooper and had handed out the ice cream (chocolate marshmallow for Amelia, cookies and cream for Didi, and rainbow swirl for Harriet) before the girls could even get their money together.

The girls were the only customers in the store, so they had their choice of tables. They opted for one at the back of the shop, near the oven, where Eleanor was baking fresh waffle cones.

Resa ate a spoonful of creamy pink ice cream, then pulled her trusty Idea Book out of her pocket. "I made a list," she announced, "of all the ways we screwed up."

"Oh, great," said Amelia with a good-natured eye roll.

"I thought this was cheer-up ice cream," said Harriet, licking her rainbow cone.

"It is," said Resa. "But it's also figure-out-what-went-wrong ice cream."

"Why? It was an epic fail, and we're definitely not doing it again," Harriet said. Resa's problem, she thought, was that she did not know how to have a good time. She wanted to work, work, work all the time. She invented work even when there was no work to be done!

"It's only an epic fail if we don't figure out what we did wrong," argued Resa. "I mean, you win some, you lose some. But if we figure out what mistakes we made, it's not a fail. It's a priceless learning opportunity." She uncapped her pen. "So come on! If we were going to do it again, what would we change?"

"The logo," said Didi, looking down at her ice cream. "I kept telling you all that we should make sure people liked it before we placed the order."

"We rushed things too much," agreed Resa, nodding. "We should've gathered more feedback beforehand."

"Yeah, but it's not like we could've sent the logo to every single person ahead of time and gotten them to vote," said Harriet.

"Sure we could've," said Amelia. "It's a little something called social media."

"We should have made a poll!" said Resa. "Joe and Sam could've posted it. They'd get tons of responses."

"We should've asked for sample shirts, too," said Amelia, her mouth full of chocolate marshmallow ice cream. "The logo printed out super small and squashed; we would've fixed that if we'd gotten a sample."

"Yeah, and also, those shirts ran really small," said Didi. "It totally messed up our orders, having to switch sizes around."

"Sample shirt. Great idea," said Resa, scribbling notes in her Idea Book.

"And honestly, we paid too much for those T-shirts," said Amelia.

Harriet started to protest, but Amelia kept on talking. "I love Lucy and all, but we should've negotiated with her. We had to make our prices too high to make any profit, and since the shirts were so expensive, not that many people wanted to buy them. Especially since they were, um, fashion-challenged."

"Right," said Resa, turning the page to continue her notes.

"I don't know how I feel about you two getting along," said Harriet suspiciously. "It was bad when you both hated each other, but now that you're mind-melding, me and Di—"

"Get even less of a say," Didi finished her friend's sentence.

Resa slid the book and pen over to Didi. "Okay," Resa said. "Your turn. What'd we do wrong?"

"Well," said Didi, drawing a decorative heading with perfect pen strokes in Resa's book, "one big problem was that we didn't have a system for pre-orders. Someone should be helping Harriet, taking down names and sizes and stuff so that we keep all that information straight."

"Yeah, and someone has to tell Joe and the other Radical Skinks they can't take preorders," Amelia added. "They can build buzz and rock out, but they need to stay away from the money."

"And, as much as I hate to admit it, Val was right about our merch table being a mess," said Didi. "It was the Wild West out there. People were just grabbing their own shirts . . . and then there was the Great Lemonade Spill."

"The second Great Lemonade Spill of the year," Resa pointed out with a smile, remembering what had happened at their lemonade stand a few weeks earlier.

"I think one person should've been in charge of handing out T-shirts," said Didi. "And that person should've been me."

The girls were surprised by Didi's confidence but glad to hear it.

"Good idea," said Amelia. "The next time we sell merch for the Radical Skinks—"

"If the Radical Skinks even exist anymore," added Harriet.

"If the Radical Skinks even exist anymore," repeated Amelia, "you should be the head honcho of the merch counter, Didi."

"The boss lady!" Harriet chirped.

"The boss lady of the *counter*," corrected Resa. "And Amelia should be the boss lady of the money."

"Can I get business cards that say that?" asked Amelia.

"Sure, you can get imaginary business cards," said Harriet, "for our imaginary next time selling merch for the imaginary band that doesn't exist anymore."

16

"Sorry for eavesdropping," said Eleanor. She'd been taking waffle cones out of the oven and was now filling one up for herself with butter pecan ice cream. "But I have a thought." Eleanor dropped the scooper in its cold-water bath. "I was at the concert, you know."

"Really?" asked Harriet. Her eyes fell on the math textbook on the counter, and she remembered where she knew Eleanor from. "Oh, that's right. You know Larry. You're his calculus lifeline."

"That's me." Cone in hand, Eleanor pushed through the swinging half door, which blocked off the counter, and pulled a chair over to the girls' table. "There's one problem you forgot to write down in that little book of yours," she said.

"What?" asked Didi, uncapping the pen.

"Customer service," said Eleanor.

"Oh," said Harriet knowingly. "You must be confused. We are *amazing* with customers. It's kind of our thing."

"Okay," said Eleanor. She took a lick of her ice cream. "If you say so."

"Harriet's right," Amelia said. "We gave out refunds. We let people switch sizes. And we didn't have to do any of that. People appreciated that."

Eleanor pulled out her phone, swiped, typed, and scrolled. Then she handed the phone to Amelia.

"'Beware the Rad Skinks tee table!'" Amelia read aloud. "'Shirts are ugly and overpriced and they insult you. Skip it!'"

Resa leaned in to look at the screen. "Who posted that?"

"'Skinks 4Eva,'" read Amelia. "But he's not the only one. There's lot of people complaining that we were rude."

Resa's mouth hung open. "*Us?* We were rude? Did you hear the customers? They were nightmares!"

"I'm not saying they weren't," said Eleanor. "They were probably obnoxious and impatient and demanding. I deal with customers every day—when we have any." She was trying to lighten the mood with a joke, but the girls didn't so much as crack a smile. "Customers can be terrible. I could tell you stories . . ." Eleanor took another lick of her cone. "But you have to be polite and professional even when they're not. You know what they say about customers . . ."

"They don't grow on trees," said Harriet.

"That is true, I guess," replied Eleanor. "But not what I was thinking."

"The customer's always right," said Amelia with a heavy sigh.

"Yep," said Eleanor. "And here's why: The only thing better than a customer is a *repeat* customer. If you're super friendly"—she plastered a big, fake smile on her face—"even when they're being unreasonable"—she made her smile bigger and tighter—"they will come back."

Eleanor relaxed her face and licked her cone.

"Like, last week, this guy comes in and orders a black cherry cone," she said. "So I scooped it fresh from the tub, right? And he takes, like, two licks and comes back. To *return* it. Says it's not cold enough."

"What?" Didi laughed. "That's ridiculous."

"I know!" said Eleanor. "He's flat-out wrong. But I just smile and say, 'Oh, I'm really sorry about that, sir. Would you like to try another flavor?' He orders the Meyer Lemon, which is in the tub *right* next to the black cherry, okay? It was absolutely, positively the same temperature. But for whatever reason, he loves this one. Perfect, great, that's the end of that, right?"

"Right," said Harriet. She hardly knew Eleanor, but she liked her. She could see right away why Larry relied on her for calculus. She was sharp.

"Wrong!" exclaimed Eleanor. "Because, get this—the next day, he comes back with his wife and three kids. Then—no joke—his wife tells her sister about the shop, and now her sister comes in every Friday with her daughter's hockey team."

"Ahhh, I see where you're going with this," said Resa, nodding.

"Of course you do, Pistachio," said Eleanor. "I could've told the guy to take a hike because he was dead wrong. I would've sold one ice cream, and that's it. Instead, I bit my tongue and tossed his black cherry cone into the trash, which led to selling dozens more cones later."

"You are a biz whiz," said Resa admiringly.

"Nah," said Eleanor. "I've just had lots of practice. You win some, you learn some. Trust me, I ran off plenty of customers when I started here."

"Did you ever tell anyone to take it up with customer service?" asked Resa.

"Way worse than that," said Eleanor. "I told some girl once, 'Buzz off, Bigmouth.'"

Resa winced.

"Yeah, and then, to make things even worse, she did buzz off, without paying." Eleanor laughed. "And I had to cover the cost of her cone out of my own paycheck.

"Not my finest moment." Eleanor shook her head. "It's a steep learning curve. You'll get the hang of it. You just have to take a lot of deep breaths and learn the magic words."

"Which are . . . ?" Amelia asked.

"'So sorry about that!' and 'It's my pleasure!'" said Eleanor. "Served up with a big smile."

The bell on the door of the shop jangled, and all five girls looked in its direction.

Joe and Sam walked in, with Larry behind them.

"Oh no," moaned Harriet. She slid down in her seat and tried to cover her face with her ponytail. She'd managed to avoid her brothers in their little house, only to run smack into them in town.

But Joe smiled brightly at the girls. "Harry! Ladies! You all got a sweet tooth, too, huh?"

Eleanor, seeing the boys, got to her feet quickly, hitting the table with her knees as she stood. The light plastic table tilted and would have fallen over if Amelia hadn't caught it. In the process, all the cups and spoons and napkins flew up in the air.

She rushed to pick up the cups and spoons. So did Larry.

"Hi," Larry said, handing her a dripping cup and dirty napkin as his cheeks turned a deep rose.

"Hi," replied Eleanor, her cheeks matching his.

Resa raised her eyebrows at Harriet, as if to say, "Really? Those two?" and Harriet gave a little shrug as if to say, "Don't look at me. I know nothing."

Eleanor tossed the garbage into the trash can and stepped behind the counter.

"What can I get for you?" she asked.

She served up a cup of s'mores for Sam, a cone of mango sorbet for Joe, and then got into a long conversation with Larry when he asked her what flavor she would recommend.

"Well, I mean, that totally depends," she said, "on a variety of factors."

While Larry and Eleanor debated flavors, Joe and Sam sat at the table next to the girls.

"Ladies, we owe you an apology," said Sam. "We blamed you for the concert, but it wasn't your fault. That amp's been glitching up for weeks."

Harriet looked down and shook her head slowly. "You're just trying to be nice. I jinxed you, Joe. You were in the zone, and I jinxed you, plain and simple."

"Harry, we were all nervous wrecks last night," Joe confessed. "That's why Sam broke the drum. That's why my voice was off. I mean, why do you think I was in the zone for so long? I was stalling. It wasn't your fault."

Harriet wanted to believe Joe, but she couldn't shake the feeling that it was all her fault. Being the youngest, she often felt as if she was the one who messed up. Her brothers seemed so capable—they had jobs and took final exams and were about to leave home for college, and she was still just a kid.

"So, do you accept our apology?" asked Sam.

Amelia, Resa, and Didi issued a chorus of "Sure!" and "Of course!" but Harriet remained silent.

"Harry looks sad," Sam said to Joe.

"Are you thinking what I'm thinking?" asked Joe.

The boys stood, grabbing Larry by the elbow as they walked around the table to Harriet.

"Sibling sandwich!" Sam yelled.

The boys surrounded their sister and gave her a big bear hug. Harriet's face lit up, and she belly-laughed as they chanted, "Har-ri-et! Har-ri-et!"

Finally, she called out, through her peals of laughter, "Okay, okay, I forgive you," and the boys quieted down.

"The Battle of the Bands would've been fun, but seriously, I need to work to save up for next year," said Sam.

"Yeah, and calculus is like a full-time job," said Larry.

"We'll try next year, when things are less busy," agreed Joe.

But Harriet knew that Sam would be away next year. They couldn't try again. It was now or never. "No!" she shouted, more loudly than she'd meant to. "You will *not* give up on your dream!"

"Harry, seriously, it's not a big deal," said Joe.

"It *is* a big deal!" she said, getting to her feet. "It's the biggest of deals. It's gigantic! It's gargantuan!"

"I like your enthusiasm," said Sam. "But we can't play in the Battle of the Bands without a guitar or drums. Joe can't sing a cappella."

Harriet was pacing now, back and forth in front of the ice-cream counter. "Larry, did you return the guitar to Music Mania yet?" she asked.

Larry, who'd been sneaking glances at Eleanor, who was busy pretending not to glance at him, stammered a bit, then said, "Uhhh, no. I was going to bring it by later today."

"Don't you *dare*!" exclaimed Harriet. "We're going to keep the guitar a little longer. In fact, we're going to borrow a drum."

The boys exchanged puzzled looks.

Joe raised his eyebrows. "Harriet, don't go overboard—"

"Oh, I'm going overboard all right." Harriet paused and laughed in a way that was almost sinister. "I'm going ker-splash into the waters. I will not stop until you are *world famous rock stars*."

Resa gasped and stood suddenly: "I know! We could—"

"Yes!" said Harriet. "At the Battle—"

"And also!" said Amelia, standing, too. "Credit cards! Because—"

"Yes! And maybe . . ." Didi piped up. "Baseball caps?"

Resa was nodding fast. "Genius. Yes. Why didn't we—"

Amelia interrupted, "But first we need to go to—"

"You're right," agreed Harriet. "I'll go with you."

"But," asked Amelia, "how will we pay for the stuff?"

"We'll cross that bridge when we come to it," said Resa. "Now, we've got to hustle."

The girls had nearly reached the front door by the time Joe called out, "Wait!"

The girls stopped and turned to face him.

"What's going on?" asked Sam.

"Didi and I are going to Music Mania," said Resa as she zipped up her hoodie. "We're going to talk to what's-her-name—"

"Mo," said Harriet.

"Yeah, Mo, and see if she'll let you borrow the guitar for another week, and also we'll see if she'll lend Sam a what's-it-called, the drum that broke?"

Sam looked bewildered but answered, "A snare."

"Good, yes, a snare," said Resa.

"And Amelia and I are going to Lucy's shop," said Harriet, "to see about placing another order—but this time, we're getting a better deal on the T-shirts."

"What shirts?" asked Larry.

"To sell at the Battle of the Bands!" replied Harriet. "Along with the baseball caps! Don't worry. We'll have a credit card reader this time."

"Baseball caps?" repeated Joe.

"Look," said Amelia, "we'd love to catch you up on everything, but it's got to be later. No time right now."

"We should meet up tonight," said Resa. "How about . . ." She looked at Amelia, Didi, and Harriet. "Want to say six? At your place, Harriet?"

"Perfect!" Harriet replied. She clapped her hands excitedly. "See you then. Bye, guys! Bye, Eleanor!"

And with that, the girls were gone.

Eleanor cracked open her calculus textbook and smiled at the brothers—at one brother in particular.

"Well," she said. "Looks like the Startup Squad has left the building."

"Hello, sweet peas!" sang Lucy as Amelia and Harriet walked through the door of Small Joys. She was standing behind the counter with a box of scarves in front of her, folding and rolling them into swirly shapes for display. "Rambo! We've got company!"

The store had one customer—an older teenage girl sitting cross-legged in the corner reading a coffee-table book about narwhals. She looked nice and comfortable, as if she'd been there awhile. She also looked unlikely to buy anything.

Rambo glanced up from his cat bed in the corner and, seeing Harriet, lazily stretched, then walked over on velvet paws to weave in between her legs.

"Ooooh, you little furball," Harriet cooed. "You want treats, don't you? Can I, Lucy?"

Lucy nodded, and Harriet leaned over the counter to fish a cat treat out of the container. Rambo licked it from her palm and then busied himself scratching his back against the corner of a bookcase.

"So how'd the shirts work out?" Lucy fiddled with a scarf knot, then looked up. "Make a lot of money?"

"Not exactly," said Harriet. She was starting to feel nervous about negotiating with Lucy. Lucy had become a friend. Could you haggle about money with a friend?

"We ran into a bunch of problems," explained Amelia, tucking her hair behind her ears. "The shirts ran really small, so all the customers wanted one size bigger, which left us with a ton of smalls and not enough larges."

"Huh," said Lucy. "I haven't heard that before. Good feedback." Unsatisfied with her scarf knot, she unrolled it and started from scratch.

Amelia elbowed Harriet and whispered, "Go ahead. Ask her."

"Actually, we wanted to see if we could place another order," said Harriet. "There's a big Battle of the Bands coming up. We want to try a do-over at that show."

"Oh yes," said Lucy. "I heard about that. People are excited. Winner's going on that singing and dancing show with that heartless judge."

"Connor Mackelvoe," said Harriet. "We love him!"

"Different strokes for different folks," said Lucy, shrugging. "So you want to place another order?"

"Yes," said Harriet at the exact same time that Amelia said, "Maybe."

"We'd like to place an order," Amelia explained. "But we need a lower price on the T-shirts. Twenty dollars each is just too high for us to make enough of a profit."

Lucy put down the scarf she was rolling and looked up at Amelia with surprise.

"Huh," she said, nodding slowly. "I'm not sure I can do any better, sweet pea. Like I told Harriet, if it's a rush order, my vendor charges an extra fee. And I've been open only a few weeks; I haven't worked with many vendors. I'm just getting started."

Harriet leaned over to scratch behind Rambo's ears. "We know, Lucy," she said. "And we're sorry to bother you."

"But maybe there's another vendor you could try," pressed Amelia. "And since you're a new customer, maybe they'll give you a promotional price for your first order and waive the rush fee."

Lucy smiled. Her eyes were twinkling. "Harriet," she said. "You've got yourself a clever business part-ner over here."

Harriet lifted Rambo in her arms. "I know," she said. "That's why I pay her the big bucks."

Lucy laughed and set her reading glasses on her nose. She pulled out the mammoth black binder, which she'd stowed under the register, and placed it on the counter with a thud. She thumbed through it, making a sucking sound with her teeth as she considered. "Ohhhhkay," she murmured as she read. "Okay, this could work."

She peered over the tops of her glasses at Amelia. "How much do you want to pay per T-shirt?"

Amelia was ready. "Twelve dollars per shirt. At the most."

"Okay," said Lucy. "I can't promise anything, but I'll try my best."

"And," Amelia continued, "we really can't pay the full amount up front. Could we put down a deposit? And pay the rest when the T-shirts arrive? That'll give us enough time to get together the money from preorders."

"You girls have really thought this through," said Lucy with admiration.

"We learned it the hard way," Harriet said.

"So all that's left is timing," said Lucy. "When do you need them by?"

"Umm, next Saturday?" Harriet ventured.

Amelia gave her an encouraging look.

"Next Saturday!" Harriet said more confidently.

"That's five business days again." Lucy grimaced. "Gonna be tight."

She turned on her cell phone and started typing in a phone number.

"You girls browse for a bit. Spoil Rambo. I'll make some calls and see what I can do for you."

Amelia walked over to the earring display, near where the high schooler was still reading.

"Hey," said the girl, letting the book rest on her lap, "you two are selling Radical Skinks T-shirts at the Battle of the Bands?"

"Uhh, yeah," replied Amelia. "That's the plan."

"Same T-shirts as last time?" asked the girl.

"No," replied Amelia. "A brand-new design this time."

"Good," said the girl. "Those last ones looked like—"

"We know, we know," said Harriet.

"Why don't you make the shirts blue?" asked the girl. "I mean, blue is the Skinks' official color. Because of the skink tongues and everything."

"Ahhhhhhhh!" Harriet let forth a groan, then hit herself in her forehead.

"Is she all right?" the girl asked Amelia.

"Oh yeah, she does this," said Amelia.

"Blue! Of course!" exclaimed Harriet. "It's like Radical Skinks trivia 101. How could we forget?"

The girl gave a little shrug and resumed reading. "That's what I'm saying."

When the girls reconvened that night at Harriet's house, they had tons of good news to share. They sat around Harriet's kitchen table, crunching on carrot sticks.

"You girls need vitamins!" Harriet's mom had said as she placed a plate of carrot sticks in the middle of the table. "I can tell by looking at your hair."

Then Mrs. Nguyen excused herself to see about dinner, and the girls swapped stories from their day.

Amelia explained that Lucy had spoken to a new vendor, who had agreed to give the girls the T-shirts at twelve dollars apiece, and—even better news—

they needed only a 50 percent deposit to place the order.

"The other half's due when the shirts are delivered, which gives us plenty of time to collect preorders," explained Amelia. "It's totally perfect. There's only one catch—the shirts have to be one size fits all."

Resa considered as she bit into a carrot stick. "That's okay," she concluded. "In fact, it's easier for us. No switching sizes."

"I think we should sell them for $19.50," said Amelia. "We'll make almost eight dollars on each shirt."

"Maybe we should round up to twenty dollars," suggested Didi. She was wearing Zappa-armor, a baseball cap with a hoodie pulled up over it, and she kept glancing over at Harriet's lap to make sure Zappa was still slumbering there. "To keep it simple."

Resa shook her head. "If we keep the price in the teens, it looks a lot lower, which'll make people want to buy. Plus, a lot of people will just tell us to keep the change, so we'll make twenty dollars on a lot of the sales."

"Exaaaaactly," said Amelia. She broke a carrot stick in half with a satisfying *snap*! Then she popped one half in her mouth.

"Did you order baseball caps?" asked Didi.

"No," said Harriet. "They didn't have any. But they

did have . . ." She unzipped her sweater to reveal no fewer than six buttons of varying sizes pinned to her yellow tunic.

"'Vote for Liptiz'?" asked Resa, reading one button and then another. "'Be bold—eat cabbage!'?"

"Yeah, Lucy had lots of samples, so she said I could have some," said Harriet. "This one's my favorite!" She pointed to a large lime-green button by her shoulder.

"'Big Guts!'" read Didi. "'Get stuffed.'"

Resa winced. "What is Big Guts?"

"Beats me!" Harriet laughed. "A restaurant? A taxidermist?"

"Whatever it is," said Didi, shuddering, "I'm staying faaaaaar away."

"We can do buttons instead of hats," said Amelia. "We'll make way more profit anyway. They'll cost us fifty cents apiece, and we can charge two dollars, maybe even $2.50."

"That's more than double," said Resa.

"It's more than triple," Amelia corrected. "And if people can't—or don't—want to spend twenty dollars for a T-shirt, they can buy buttons. Or they can buy both."

"Buttons are also good advertising for the Radical Skinks," said Resa. "Because people can leave the buttons on their backpacks or jackets, where everyone can see the band name."

"We should have them right up front on the table, so customers can just grab them and buy them before they even have a chance to think about it," suggested Harriet. "Like how they always have candy bars by the register at the supermarket."

"An impulse buy," said Resa.

"Right!" agreed Harriet. "You buy them without thinking because they look so good. And they're only a dollar, and before you know it, you're sinking your teeth into a luscious, creamy, chocolaty—"

"Here," interrupted Didi, handing her a carrot. "Eat this. You seem hungry."

"Did someone say *hungry*?" sang Mrs. Nguyen, sailing into the room. "Dinner's in five minutes!" She turned to Harriet and noticed the carrot stick, untouched, in her hand. "Eat that carrot! You need Vitamin D . . . or C . . . or whatever's in carrots."

Harriet obliged with a tiny nibble, though she wore a look of extreme disgust on her face. She gulped loudly, and Mrs. Nguyen, satisfied, returned to the living room.

"Blegh!" Harriet said as soon as her mother had left the room. "Raw vegetables are the worst. There's nothing to mask their revolting flavor."

"Lucy's in the store tomorrow morning," said Amelia. "So if we get her the design by noon, she'll send it to the vendor, and they should be able to get us the shirts by Friday afternoon."

"I already came up with three options for new logos," said Didi. "But I need to know what color the T-shirt is going to be before I add color."

"Blue!" said Harriet. "Because . . ." She picked up Zappa and held the carrot about an inch in front of her face; the skink darted her blue tongue out to lick it.

"Good girl!" said Harriet, placing Zappa, and the carrot stick, on her lap.

Didi scooted her chair back reflexively. Reptiles were always her kryptonite, but especially when their tongues were visible. She took a big breath and refocused on the subject at hand. "What shade of blue do we want the T-shirts to be?" she asked. "Azure? Cerulean? Indigo?"

"How about whatever you call this?" Amelia opened up a photo on her phone and showed it to Didi. "It's the only blue the vendor offers."

"Okay, midnight blue, got it," said Didi. "I'll add color to my logo ideas after dinner. I brought my sketchbook."

"We have good news, too," said Resa. She drum-rolled her toes and looked at the girls expectantly.

"Well?" asked Amelia. "What's the good news?"

Resa drum-rolled her toes again.

"You know you're supposed to follow that with a big announcement, right?" asked Amelia. "That's how a drumroll works."

Resa rolled her eyes. "The drumroll *is* the news! We got Sam a loaner snare drum! And Larry can keep the guitar one more week. The boys are at Music Mania now, picking up the drum."

"Winner, winner, chicken dinner!" yelled Harriet.

Zappa looked up suddenly from her carrot, causing Didi to yell, "Grab the skink!" Harriet clamped a hand down on Zappa's back, keeping her in place.

Harriet beamed. "We've got a good system now, Di."

Didi didn't look so sure.

"So what'd you have to give to that shark Mo?" asked Amelia suspiciously.

Resa shrugged. "Not much. Just four shout-outs a day on social media; a promise to buy the drum and the guitar at her shop; a free T-shirt; and, if the Radical Skinks win the Battle of the Bands, they have to thank Music Mania on national television."

Amelia whistled. "At least you didn't have to give her your firstborn child."

Resa tilted her chin down at Amelia. "What can I tell you? She's tough, that Mo. She knows she's got all the cards. We're at her mercy."

"What about an amp?" asked Harriet.

Resa shook her head. "No go. But the boys have a friend who's good with electronics, and she was able to fix the cord—for the time being. It'll hold up for one more show."

There was a knock at the door, followed by Mrs. Nguyen's yelling, "I've got it!" A minute later, a delicious aroma wafted into the room.

Harriet inhaled deeply. "Smells like—"

"Dinner!" announced Mrs. Nguyen as she walked in, two boxes of pizza stacked in her hands.

Harriet squealed in excitement. "One of the best things about pizza," she said, opening the first box, "is that it gets the gross taste of carrots out of your mouth."

Joe and Sam posted Didi's three logo options later that night, and within an hour there was a clear winner.

Option two won by a landslide: simple block letters, all in very pale blue, spelling the band name, with the *I* in *SKINKS* made into a stand holding a retro microphone.

Sam said it was classy.

Joe said it was classic.

Larry said it reminded him of a Sandy Warhol painting.

The girls were just glad to have a clear consensus

so that they could show customers a picture when they took preorders.

The easiest time to take preorders was right after dismissal in front of the high school, but they couldn't wait that long; they needed cash in hand to give Lucy half of the order amount by Monday morning.

Lucky for them, the high school was putting on a production of the school play, *The Music Man*, on Sunday afternoon, and that event drew a big crowd. Harriet and Didi dragged a card table to the corner of the high school, about a half hour before the play started.

With Harriet's mouth behind a megaphone and Didi's design mounted on a sign, they rustled up just enough orders Sunday to give Lucy her deposit.

Didi was in charge of taking down information for preorders this time. She came equipped with her laptop so that she could enter the names directly into a spreadsheet, which she could keep alphabetized and back up on the cloud. There was no chance it would be lost or damaged.

It was a tight operation. Harriet got people interested, especially friends of her brothers, and then she sent them over to Didi to pay. A few people griped about how terrible the last T-shirts were and asked if the Radical Skinks had broken their curse, but Harriet didn't take any of it personally. She just deflected the tension with a joke about how they'd gotten a counterhex, so all was good now.

She was able to keep up her good humor all week, and by the end of it, most of the unhappy fans were willing to give the Radical Skinks—and their T-shirts—another try.

〰〰〰〰

On Friday at lunch, Harriet called Lucy to see if the T-shirt order had arrived.

"Sorry, sweet pea, not yet," said Lucy regretfully. "But it's still early. Check back after school."

"There goes my social studies quiz," said Harriet to the girls when she hung up. "I can't possibly focus on Mesopotamia! All I'm thinking about is that if we don't get the shirts tonight, we won't have anything to sell tomorrow at the Battle of the Bands!"

"Harriet," said Didi sternly, "you have got to calm down."

"Do fifty jumping jacks," suggested Resa. "That's what I do when I need to clear my head. Works like a charm."

Harriet, who wasn't much of an athlete, could manage only eleven, but it helped. She made it through social studies and math, and by the time she got out of music class, she was feeling optimistic again.

After school, Resa and Amelia had tennis lessons,

★ 143 ★

so Didi and Harriet rushed to Small Joys, where Lucy told them if they wanted to pick up their order, they'd have to work for it.

"See that stack?" Lucy gestured at a tall pile of boxes by the front door. "They all just got delivered. You open them for me, I bet you'll find your order."

"Box cutter!" barked Harriet, her palm open in front of her like a surgeon in need of a scalpel.

They sliced open what felt like a dozen boxes with no luck and were beginning to despair by the time they came to the bottom box in the pile.

Didi slid the X-Acto knife through the packing tape on top, pulled open the box, and saw heaps of midnight blue fabric. "Jackpot!" she called to Harriet, who'd gotten distracted by a box of hair accessories she'd opened.

As Harriet ran over, Didi unfolded a T-shirt and held it at arm's length.

Harriet screeched so loudly it was a wonder the windows in the shop didn't shatter.

"It's utter perfection!" exclaimed Harriet. "A masterpiece! You're a *genius!*" She threw her arms around Didi's slight shoulders and squeezed so hard Didi couldn't breathe.

"Satisfied customers," said Lucy from behind the counter, with Rambo in her arms. "My favorite kind."

20

The Battle of the Bands was scheduled for noon
Saturday at the high school auditorium, but audience members started lining up by eleven o'clock.
There had been a regular Battle of the Bands at the
high school for as long as Harriet could remember, and while it was always pretty popular, it never
drew a crowd this big. Everyone had heard about
the destiny of this year's winner, and everybody in
town—young, old, and in-between—wanted to be
there to witness the competition.

"Do you think Connor Mackelvoe's gonna be
here?" asked Didi, bubbling over with excitement.

The girls had arrived with all their stuff a full hour early and had been allowed into the auditorium only when they explained they were staff. "We handle the Radical Skinks' merchandise," Harriet had said with pride, and magically they were waved through.

Each of the six bands performing was allowed one merch table in the back of the auditorium. They'd been warned they could sell before the show only, not after, and absolutely no voice-amplifying devices were allowed.

"Meaning?" Harriet had asked the concert organizer who was explaining the rules.

"Meaning you can put that megaphone away," she'd said. "If I catch you on it, I'm shutting down your operation."

Amelia had grabbed the megaphone out of Harriet's hands. "Won't be a problem!" she promised.

Now all four girls stood in a line behind the merch table, ready, willing, and able to make merch history. They all wore a bona fide Radical Skinks tee, one size fits all. The shirt was a little big on Harriet and Resa, the smallest girls in the group, so Resa had cut the extra fabric off the bottom of hers, folding it into a headband to keep her curls out of her face. Harriet, inspired by Amelia, had tied her too-big shirt into a knot at her hip.

Didi had her laptop all fired up and her master

list in alphabetical order. She'd printed out a stack of copies of her list, in case she lost power, but had instructed the girls to keep their hands off her list. "Don't forget; I'm queen of this counter," she said. "Now follow me."

She led the girls directly in front of the table and gestured to the two signs she'd hung on opposite ends of the rectangular table. One sign read PREORDERS and another read BUY NOW.

"Two lines!" Didi announced. "One for people who already paid and one for people who want to buy now. I'm in charge of preorders, and Amelia is in charge of buy now."

"Got it, Captain," said Harriet with a little salute.

"So if your name is not Didi or Amelia," said Didi, giving Resa and Harriet a hard stare, "you should not lay a finger on the T-shirts."

"What about buttons?" asked a voice from behind Didi.

It was Val. For once, she was not wearing sequins, just a plain old black hoodie with black sweats.

"Val," said Resa, instantly annoyed, "we don't have time for pestering."

"It's a real question," said Val. "Who's in charge of buttons?"

"I didn't think of that . . ." said Didi.

"I can help," Val chimed in. "If you want."

"No," Resa answered quickly. "We're all set."

"You weren't all set last time," said Val with a shrug. "I'm just trying to help."

"Really?" said Resa. "The way you helped last week when you conned Harriet into getting autographs for your T-shirt so you could sell it for double what you paid?"

Val blinked fast, looking surprised.

"Yeah, we know all about your schemes," said Harriet, crossing her arms.

"It wasn't a scheme," said Val. "I didn't lie or anything. And I didn't steal any of your customers, because you weren't even offering autographed T-shirts. I provided a service you didn't have. You should be thanking me."

"You don't even like the Radical Skinks!" protested Harriet. "You just want to make a buck!"

"I'm not in it for the *money*!" said Val, anger flashing in her green eyes.

"Then why are you all up in our business?" asked Resa.

"I think it's cool, all right?" Val said with a scowl. "I love this kind of thing, but you all never even think of asking me to help."

"Wait," said Didi, "are you serious? You really just want to help?"

Val shrugged. "Yeah," she said so quietly they almost couldn't hear her.

"Resa?" asked Didi expectantly.

The girls had been best friends for long enough that Resa knew what Didi wanted her to do without her having to say anything. She hooked her arm through Didi's and pulled her to the side of the table for a private conference.

"Are you kidding me?" Resa whispered. "You know she's impossible to work with!"

"So are you," Didi teased. "But that doesn't stop me from being your best friend."

"I'm being serious," Resa replied.

"She's not impossible," Didi said. "She's just, well, assertive about her ideas—like you. And just like you, she's got a lot of good ideas."

Resa pulled her blue headband down off her hairline and then readjusted it in place. "The autographed T-shirts are actually a smart idea." She made a clicking sound on the back of her teeth as she considered. "Fine. On a trial basis."

Didi grinned and gave Resa's shoulders a little, approving squeeze. Then she walked back over to the table. "Val—"

"Just hear me out, would you?" Val was insistent. "You could get the boys to sign, like, five ahead of time, now, and have them up here. You could sell them for a lot more than the rest. You could say there's a limited supply."

"That's a great idea," Didi said.

"It is?" replied Val. "I mean, thanks."

"I have a great idea, myself," said Didi.

Didi grabbed a shirt from the pile on the table and handed it to Val.

"Put it on," she encouraged. "So people will know you're with us."

Val turned to Resa, her eyes opened wide. "Seriously?"

Resa sighed. "On a trial basis."

A kind of giggle started to erupt from Val's throat, which she immediately suppressed. "Cool," she said, trying her best to be casual. "I guess I can help. I mean, since you really need me."

Resa rolled her eyes. She whispered to Didi, "If she's a disaster, I'm never doing anything nice for anyone again."

"That's reasonable," Didi joked.

Resa turned her attention to double-checking that the credit card reader app and device on her cell phone were working properly, while Harriet ran backstage with five T-shirts to get the boys' autographs.

The auditorium had a real stage, with an actual—but worn—red curtain and a big backstage area to boot. There was even a Battle of the Bands staff member at the entrance to the backstage area, barring people from entering. Harriet told the man she was the Skinks' sister and also their tour manager, but he kept shaking his head, his face expressionless.

Just as Harriet was about to lose her cool, Joe,

returning from the restroom, arrived on the scene. "She's with the band," he said. And just like that, Harriet was in.

"Thanks, bro," said Harriet. "Is it okay I'm here? I don't want to disturb you."

Joe slung his arm around Harriet's shoulders. "Relax, sis. I'm taking a break from the zone. I think it was stressing me out more than relaxing me."

Harriet caught sight of the yellow T-shirt Joe was wearing under his black leather jacket.

"You're wearing a Music Mania shirt for the show?" she asked, surprised.

"Yeah, Mo made me agree to that before she'd hand over the loaner drum," he said. "I don't really care. Fashion is an illusion."

Harriet furrowed her brows. "Bite your tongue!"

The backstage area was loud and crowded. Joe gave Harriet a quick tour of the competition as they passed each band.

There was Tricky Vulture, an all-girl punk rock band, and Two Is Better Than One, a boyfriend/girlfriend folk duo. There was Smash!, a glam rock band who seemed to have more makeup on their faces than everyone in the audience combined. There was Armageddon Town, a heavy metal group. Then there was the last contender, a band with eight members, all of them lying in a circle on the floor with their eyes closed.

"Who're they?" Harriet asked Joe in a whisper as they walked past the group. The youngest looked about Harriet's age, and the oldest looked as if she might be a grandmother. Every band member wore all white, and they were barefoot. Diagonally across their chests, they wore beauty pageant–style banners, which read, in blue sparkly letters, XPECTATION!

"Ah, Xpectation!" said Joe with a wry smile. "They're an experimental rock band from downtown."

"Where are their instruments?" asked Harriet.

"They don't have any," said Joe. "Their whole thing is, they pick up whatever's lying around and make music with that."

"I don't want to jinx you, but looking at your competition, I think you guys have a really good shot!" Harriet said, giddy with excitement as Joe led her to the Radical Skinks' corner of the backstage. She was surprised to find Eleanor there, adjusting the collar on Larry's retro bowling shirt.

"Are they a thing?" Harriet asked Joe.

"Not officially." Joe nodded in Larry and Eleanor's direction. "But I mean, it sure looks like it."

Harriet got her brothers to autograph the T-shirts and sped back to the merch table so she could rustle up new customers. As it turned out, there was no need. The Radical Skinks' merch table had the longest line of all the tables by far. So many customers wanted to buy T-shirts on the spot that Resa told Harriet to stop advertising and start accepting money. When Harriet reached over to give her first customer a T-shirt, Didi grabbed her hand.

"Is your name Amelia or Didi?" she asked.

"Resa told me to help," protested Harriet. "Look at the line! Even Disneyland doesn't have lines this long!"

Didi narrowed her eyes as she considered. "Fine," she said. "But you don't hand over T-shirts until you have the money in the cashbox, or until the credit card reader screen says 'confirmed'! And don't mess up my piles!"

"I promise," said Harriet.

Val was right; the autographed T-shirts sold out almost immediately. And Resa and Amelia had been right, too; most customers were in such a hurry to find a good spot to watch the show that they didn't bother waiting for change. The buttons were a huge hit, too, with some customers buying three or four at a time.

With ten minutes left until showtime, the Radical Skinks' merch table still had a long line of customers. The girls were moving as quickly as they could to take money and hand out merch, and Harriet was glad they'd accepted Val's help. She was fast and surprisingly friendly, too; way friendlier than she was in class. Her smile may have been fake, but the customers were buying it, and they were leaving with smiles on their faces, too.

Inspired by Val's example, Harriet decided to push her own charm into turbo gear. When the next customer stepped up, her smile was extra-strength. "Well, hello there! How can I help you?" she asked.

Her smile was not met with a smile in response. It was Reginald.

"Reg!" Harriet sang. "How's it going?"

He scowled. "Reginald. It's Reginald."

"Sorry!" said Harriet. "It's great to see you again!"

"Uh-huh," he grunted. He glanced over at the T-shirts. "These look a lot better than the last ones. I'll take three. And three buttons, too."

"Three T-shirts, three buttons! Coming right up!" Harriet chirped. "Cash or credit?"

Reginald handed over a credit card, and Harriet rushed it over to Resa.

Resa shook her head. "Can't. The credit card reader is down."

"What?" asked Harriet, eyes wide.

Amelia turned in Harriet's direction. "It's the Wi-Fi. I just heard the people at the Tricky Vulture merch table complaining about it. No one's able to take credit cards."

Harriet froze. "We need to get it back up!"

"Right, because it's so easy!" Resa snapped. "Forget it." She turned abruptly and stormed off.

"This is a disaster!" Harriet moaned, dropping her head into her hands. "We have only a few minutes left before the show starts, and a lot of these people don't have cash!"

"Helloooo?" called Reginald, still waiting on the other side of the table.

Harriet spun around to face him, her mournful expression transforming instantly into a cheerful grin.

"Can you speed it up?" Reginald asked, irritated. "I need to get a good seat."

"So sorry, Reg," she said. "Can you pay in cash? We're just having the teeniest bit of trouble with our credit card machine."

"No, I don't have cash!" Reginald scrunched his nose like *cash* was a distasteful word.

"You're right," said Harriet. "Just a sec!" She turned around to face Amelia, her smile dropping into a frown, like someone had pulled a lever on her mouth. She'd tried so hard to make sure everything went smoothly today, but even so, it was turning into a disaster, just like last time. "Now what do we do?"

"Gimme a minute," said Amelia. "I'm thinking."

"Well, think faster!" Harriet hissed. She wiped sweat from her brow.

"I'll go ask the show organizer about the Wi-Fi," said Amelia. "I bet they can reboot it."

"Already done!" panted Resa, reappearing on the other side of the table. She was out of breath but smiling. "They're restarting the router. And, in case that doesn't work . . ."

"What?" asked Harriet.

Resa scrambled onto a folding chair and stood, cupping her hands around her mouth to be heard over the roar of the crowd. *"We're fixing the Wi-Fi, but for now we are cash only. There's an ATM machine across the street in the deli. And don't worry! The show isn't starting for another ten minutes!"*

Harriet threw her arms around Resa's calves and lifted her up. "Three cheers for Resa!" she shouted.

"Careful!" Resa said, but she was laughing, her brown eyes twinkling.

Harriet put Resa's feet back down on the chair and darted over to where Reginald was waiting. "You wanna wait for the Wi-Fi, Reg, or hit up the ATM?"

"What if you sell out of the shirts while I go get the money?" he asked.

"I'll tell you what, Reg." Harriet leaned over and whispered conspiratorially, "I'm not doing this for anyone else, but seeing as you're our best customer and also how we didn't do right by you last time, I'm gonna put three shirts *and* three buttons to the side for you while you go to the ATM. How's that sound?"

"Cool," he said. "Skinks for"—he held four fingers up—"ever."

Harriet smiled and held four fingers up, too. "Skinks forever!"

The Wi-Fi never kicked back on strongly enough to run the credit card reader. That was okay, though, because the T-shirts sold out before the Battle of the Bands even started.

Didi had the idea to start a list for back orders, taking down names and email addresses, so that the Startup Squad could get in touch when a new shipment of T-shirts came in. And Harriet had the idea to offer a 15 percent discount on back orders if people paid right then and there.

Pretty much everyone who had cash took the discount and paid in advance.

"And if you want to show your support for the Radical Skinks right now," Harriet told each back-ordering fan, "we've got plenty of buttons for sale!"

So they sold out of buttons by the time the show started, too.

"I wish we'd ordered more T-shirts!" Harriet lamented as the last customer walked away from the table.

"We couldn't order more," Amelia reminded her. "We needed a deposit of fifty percent up front. We barely had enough to cover this amount of T-shirts."

"And besides," said Resa, "it would have been way worse to order too many T-shirts and not sell them. That way, we'd have lost money."

"I guess," said Harriet. She couldn't help but wonder if she'd done a good enough job, done everything she could to make the table a success. Things had definitely turned out better than last time—but was that really saying much?

Didi put an arm around Harriet's shoulder—and turned Harriet's body toward the audience, who were waiting for the first band to start playing. The emcee had given a short introduction and announced the randomly chosen lineup (the Radical Skinks were fifth), and now Tricky Vulture was plugging in, tuning up, and getting settled.

"Look, Harriet," Didi said, pointing toward the crowd.

Harriet had been so busy handing out merch and making change that she hadn't even glanced at the growing crowd in the auditorium. The large room was chock-full, with every seat taken and tons of people leaning against the walls. It was a sea of people. But that wasn't the most incredible part. The most incredible part was that the sea of people was midnight blue.

It wasn't all blue. But it mostly was. Harriet's eyes scanned over one pair of shoulders after another, clad in Radical Skinks T-shirts. The crowd was jammed with Skinks fans, and, when Harriet's brothers took the stage and looked out over the crowd, they'd see it. So would the judges.

"You did good, Harry," said Resa, giving her a playful elbow jab. "You did good."

Harriet smiled. "*We* did good. If it hadn't been for you and your tough love, I'd probably still be pouting in bed."

"That's what business associates are for," said Resa, shrugging.

"And friends," Didi chimed in.

"*Five! Six! Five six seven eight!*" The drummer for Tricky Vulture was hitting her drumsticks together, counting down for her band. The show was about to start.

22

The Radical Skinks were dazzling. The amp, which Harriet worried about the whole time, held up perfectly. Sam was a blur at the drums, darting his hands between the different parts of the drum kit so fast the human eye could hardly process it. Joe was pitch-perfect—his voice velvet, but with a ragged edge that made the crowd go wild. And Larry wasn't exaggerating when he said the ChromaChord 3000 gave him magical musical powers. Maybe he wasn't quite Hendrix, but he was better than he'd ever been, better than Harriet ever imagined he could be. What made their performance truly transcendent, though, was how in sync they were—as if they weren't three separate people playing three separate instruments but one mythical musical creature with three sets of arms and legs.

It wasn't just the Startup Squad who thought the Radical Skinks hit a home run. The crowd in the auditorium was locked in to the Radical Skinks' performance, cheering and clapping and singing along. When Larry played the final chord of the final song, and Sam hit the cymbals for the last time, the crowd spontaneously began to chant, *"Rad Skinks! Rad Skinks! Rad Skinks!"*

When their performance was over, Harriet sizzled with excitement. "I really don't want to jinx it, but I think they are gonna win! How could they not?"

"They're definitely the crowd favorite," said Amelia. "That's gotta count for something."

The Radical Skinks were a hard act to follow, so Xpectation!, which performed after them, had an uphill battle. They walked onto the stage, barefoot, with empty hands. They asked the audience for donations of items—anything, they said, absolutely anything, because there was nothing they could not make musical—and the audience obliged, tossing up candy bar wrappers, shoes, books, and even some Radical Skinks buttons. The band members distributed these "instruments," and, after counting down from ten like NASA Mission Control, they began to sing.

The band had no lead singer. Instead, they all sang, in unison, these words:

> *"My belly rumbles*
> *I want a sandwich*
> *The time is midnight,*
> *The time is noon,*
> *The time is never.*
> *Are you a turkey?*
> *Turtles are the loneliiiiiiiiiiiiiiest . . .*
> *animals."*

The youngest member of the band slammed a shoe down on the stage once, twice, three times. Then, silence.

The audience remained quiet, trying to decide if that was the song's finale or if there'd be more. When nothing else happened, the crowd began to clap, most of them quietly, politely. There was, however, a cluster of audience members seated toward the front, dressed all in white, with white fedoras, and those people began to whoop and whistle and cheer. The fans of Xpectation! were small in number but clearly very devoted.

"The judges will now vote," announced the emcee. "And while we wait, we'll be treated to a short acrobatic routine by a performer I hear is a real dynamo." As he was speaking, two high schoolers dragged a large blue gymnastics mat to the middle of the stage. "Let's hear it for . . . the Blaze!"

Loud, pulsating techno music blared from the auditorium's speaker system, so fast and insistent that the audience couldn't help but clap along to the beat. After a few seconds, a girl ran full speed from the wings and executed a string of gymnastic moves Harriet did not know the names for but involved flips—forward and backward—and no-handed cartwheels and one-handed handstands and all kinds of other incredible feats that defied gravity. The girl moved so fast and her leotard was so sparkly from the golden sequins that covered it that it took a minute before Harriet recognized her.

"Is that . . ." she ventured. "*Val?*"

Resa leaned forward and squinted. "Holy moly," she said. "It is."

Val did a final move—a backflip with no hands—and raised both arms above her head triumphantly as her chest moved rapidly up and down from her exertion.

"Did you know she was, like, an Olympic gymnast?" asked Amelia.

"I didn't even know she could do a cartwheel,"

marveled Harriet, shaking her head. "That girl has more tricks up her sleeve than a magician."

The girls clapped energetically along with the rest of the audience as Val gave a deep bow before running off the stage. The emcee returned to the microphone to say it'd be just one more minute.

"I can't take it," said Harriet, hiding her face in her hands.

Resa was swiping at her phone and smiling. "Wow," she said.

"A good wow or a bad wow?" asked Didi.

"Good," said Resa. "People have been posting from the show, and everybody says the Radical Skinks are gonna win."

"Really?" asked Harriet.

"And remember Skinks 4Eva, who wrote that rude post about us?" she asked. "Listen to what he just posted."

She read: " 'Love the cool new Skinks merch!!! New staff way better. Just upped my order to 3 shirts and 3 buttons. Skinks 4Eva!' "

Harriet looked at Resa, her eyes wide. "Reginald? He's Skinks 4Eva?"

"Looks like it," Resa said, nodding. "And he's in our corner now."

"Ladies and gentlemen!" The emcee was back at the mic. "We have a winner!"

The crowd grew silent.

"As everybody knows, this is a very *special* Battle of the Bands," the emcee continued.

"Amazing contenders, every one. It was an incredibly close vote for the judges, so close we had to do a recount."

Harriet's stomach felt as if there were some kind of animal trapped in there doing somersaults. She couldn't take the anticipation.

"But finally," the emcee went on, "we have the results!"

Harriet squeezed her eyes shut and balled her hands into fists. "Pleasepleasepleaseplease," she whispered under her breath.

"The winner of tonight's Battle of the Bands . . ."

Harriet felt a hand reach for hers. She opened her fists and clasped Didi's fingers. Then, on her other side, another hand, this one belonging to Resa. On Harriet's shoulder, she felt Amelia's hands giving a little, encouraging squeeze.

"The band who will be featured on *American Supahstars* . . ." called the emcee, "iiiiiiiiiiis . . . Xpectation!"

Harriet opened her mouth to let forth the most earsplitting whoop ever. But before she unleashed it, she realized her brothers had not, in fact, won.

The audience clapped, though it mostly came from the contingent in white fedoras toward the front of the auditorium. The members of Xpectation! were triumphant, though, grabbing any loose objects within reach—a notebook, a plastic cup, an orange traffic cone to mark off-limits areas—and banging them on nearby surfaces as they walked onstage to accept the trophy.

Harriet couldn't watch. She let go of Didi's and Resa's hands, shook Amelia's hands off her shoulder, and spun to face the wall so that they wouldn't see her eyes fill up with tears. It was embarrassing to cry in front of other people, but she couldn't help it. She'd been so sure her brothers would win. They were so talented, and the crowd loved them so much. It didn't seem fair that after all the hurdles they'd jumped through—the broken guitar, the broken drum, the broken-up band—that this is how it would end: losing to a band that didn't even have *instruments*.

"Oh, Harriet," Didi murmured. "I'm sorry."

Harriet wiped her eyes with the end of her shirt. "I know you are." Harriet sniffed. "It's not your fault."

"They were robbed," said Resa, her eyes flashing. "We should demand a recount."

"They already did a recount," Amelia pointed out.

"A re-recount," Resa demanded.

"I used to go to a ton of these contests—music, art, writing—when my mom was on the arts beat back in the city," said Amelia. "Lots of times they give the prize to the ones who are the most unique, the most outside the box. Sometimes they're great, and sometimes they're just . . ."

"Bizarre," offered Didi.

"Yeah," said Amelia. "And if the winners are going to be on national TV, they probably want them to be as bizarre as possible. I mean, sometimes people like to watch bad performances more than good ones."

"Ladies!"

Joe was jogging toward them, sweaty from performing, his face aglow. A few steps behind him was Sam, still holding his drumsticks, his hair impressively intact.

Harriet took a deep, shaky breath. She'd have to put on a brave face for her brothers. They were probably devastated.

"Did you hear our set?" asked Joe, pushing his long hair out of his eyes.

Harriet nodded. "You guys were amazing. I'm sorry—" Her voice broke off.

"You mean, 'cause we didn't win that spot on *American SupahCheesefest*?" Sam snorted with disdain. "Who cares? That's not where serious music acts perform, Harriet."

"Yeah, we were never that keen on being on that show," said Joe. "You just seemed so jazzed, we went along with it."

"And hey, any chance to play, right?" asked Sam.

"But it was good we came," said Joe, "because—Harry, you're gonna flip when you hear this."

Harriet's pulse quickened. "What?"

"There was a guy from New Blue in the audience!" Joe was so overcome with excitement, he laughed out loud.

"What's New Blue?" asked Harriet.

"A record label." It was Eleanor's voice. She'd walked up beside Harriet, and next to her, with his arm around her shoulders, was Larry.

"A really cool label," Larry added. "And he liked our set. A lot. We're going into the city next week to play him some of our stuff."

Harriet said nothing. She was absolutely dumbfounded. Her brother's dreams were literally coming true.

"We want you to handle all our merch from now on," said Sam.

"Are you game?" asked Joe.

Harriet looked from Joe to Sam to Larry. Then she inhaled deeply, raising her shoulders nearly to her ears. "*Yeeeeeeees*," she hollered. "Yes! Yes yes! Yes yes yes yes yes yes!"

Harriet ran full throttle over to Joe, flinging her arms around him. Then she did the same to Sam, and finally Larry. Eleanor leaped backward to avoid getting knocked over.

"*I saved everything! I am a star-maker!*" Harriet shouted.

Sam laughed. "Well, you *and* your associates."

"Come on, ladies and gents," said Eleanor, nodding toward the exit. "I'll use my employee discount and hook you up with ice cream."

"We actually gotta run the drum and guitar back to Music Mania," said Larry.

"Right now?" asked Eleanor.

"Yeah," said Sam. "Mo already texted me. News travels fast, and she isn't happy we didn't win. She was really counting on that shout-out on TV we promised her, so she suddenly ran out of generosity."

"I've got a better idea," said Amelia with a wry smile. "Why don't you guys go to Music Mania . . . but keep the instruments. Give her this instead." She handed Larry an overstuffed fanny pack.

"Is that the money we made?" asked Sam, eyes wide.

Amelia nodded.

"Is it enough for a guitar?" asked Larry hopefully.

"Yep," said Amelia. "And not just any guitar. It's enough to get you the ChromaChord 3000."

"Yes!" exclaimed Larry. "Yes! Yes! Yes!" He lifted Eleanor off her feet and spun her around in a circle. She beamed.

"Will there be anything left over for a drum?" Sam looked more hopeful than a little kid first thing on Christmas morning.

Amelia nodded. "That snare drum's all yours."

Now it was Sam's turn to celebrate, lifting Joe off his feet and spinning him around in a circle.

"Dude." Joe laughed, shoving his brother away playfully. "Cut it out."

"I was hoping you guys would have enough to buy a new amp, too," said Amelia. "But the rest of the money has to go toward a deposit for the next batch of T-shirts."

"Once you guys get a record deal, I have a feeling you'll be able to get an amp," said Eleanor.

"Record deal," reflected Joe. "I like the sound of that."

"Guys," said Sam to his brothers. "Should we—"

"Yeah!" said Joe. Turning to the girls, he said, "We put together a little something for you. We're going a cappella here so, you know, bear with us."

Sam hit his drumsticks together three times and then played a simple beat on the edge of the merch table. Then, in furiously fast unison, all three boys sang:

> *"You'll be wowed and awed*
> *By the Startup Squad*
> *Let's hear it for these ladies!*

They're tough and they're smart
Make you wanna applau-aud!
Let's hear it for these ladies!
They never give up easy
Even when they maybe should.
They're never mean or sleazy.
They're honest and they're good.
They're whizzes at the bizzes!
Go hire them, you should!
Oh oh oh oh ohhhhhhh
Let's hear it for these ladies!"

The boys struck a "ta-da!" pose, making it clear the song was done. The four girls—plus Eleanor—clapped and laughed.

"Come on, guys," said Sam, tugging on Larry's arm. "I don't want to get another text from Mo."

As the Radical Skinks headed off to Music Mania, Eleanor turned to the Startup Squad. "My offer still stands," she said. "Wanna get some celebratory ice cream?"

"Uhhh, I think the only question that remains," said Harriet, "is how many scoops? And can we get marshmallows on top? Jumbo ones, if possible?"

Eleanor laughed. "That's more than one question."

"It'd be good to have a meeting," said Resa, nodding. "We can figure out how big our next order should be. And if we should maybe mix it up with different colors for the shirts."

"It would be cool to make patches, too," said Didi. "You know, the kind you sew onto your backpack?"

"And do the Radical Skinks have a website?" asked Amelia. "Because they really should."

Eleanor laughed as the girls grabbed their shopping bags and boxes of supplies. "Hey," she said, gesturing under the table. "Don't forget your megaphone."

Harriet lunged for the bright orange megaphone before the other girls could stop her.

"*The Startup Squad foreva!*" she boomed.

Welcome to

THE STARTUP SQUAD

You can start your own business by yourself or form a Startup Squad with your friends! You could even sell T-shirts, like Resa, Harriet, Didi, and Amelia did for the Radical Skinks. The girls learned about *revenue*, *expense*, *profit*, *negotiation*, and *customer service* as they worked together to make money for the band. Here are some tips from the Startup Squad that will help make your own business a huge success!

Revenue is the money a customer pays you for your products. **Expense** is the money you spend to make your products. **Profit** is revenue minus expenses. It's the money you get to keep after running your business. For example, the Startup Squad sold each T-shirt for $25—that was their revenue. It cost them $20 to make each shirt—that was their expense—so their profit on each shirt was $5 ($25 - $20 = $5).

Revenue and Profit Tips

★ Make sure you're earning a profit on each item you sell. First, add up all the money you spent to make your product; that's your total expenses. For example, to sell lemonade, you need to buy lemons, sugar, and cups. Check your recipe to see how many cups of lemonade you can make. Then do some simple math to figure out how much it costs you to make each cup:

Lemonade Expenses

6 lemons	$ 4.00
1 cup of sugar	$ 1.00
1 package of cups	$ 5.00
Total expenses	$ 10.00
Cups of lemonade in each batch	10
Cost per cup of lemonade	$ 1.00

★ Once you know what each item costs to make, you can set your price to make sure you earn a profit. A good guide is to set your price at twice what it costs you to make each item. (For example, charge $2 for a cup of lemonade that costs $1 to make, so you can earn $1 in profit on each cup.) But you should also do a little research about what similar products cost—and think about what you'd be willing to pay. The Startup Squad thought that $2.50 was a fair price for a button even though the buttons cost only $0.50 to make.

★ Avoid using round numbers in your prices. $9.99 sounds less expensive than $10.00 even though it's only one penny less. Also, if you charge $1.75 for a cup of lemonade, your customers might give you two dollars and tell you to "keep the change."

★ If you're raising money for a charity or a good cause, consider not setting a price at all. Tell people to pay what they want as a donation. You might find that some people will give you a lot more money for your product than the price you were thinking of charging.

Negotiation is a way to reach an agreement. When your bedtime is eight o'clock, but you ask to stay up until nine o'clock, and you're then allowed to stay up until eight thirty, that's a negotiation! The same thing happens in business (but usually about prices, not bedtimes).

?! Negotiation Tips

★ It never hurts to politely ask someone for a lower price. The worst that can happen is the person will say no. Lucy's T-shirts were priced too high for the Startup Squad to make enough profit. Amelia asked if there was a way to get a lower price—and Lucy agreed! If you are buying a lot of something, often you can get a discount. Just ask!

★ On the flip side, if someone is thinking about buying a lot of *your* products, you might offer them a discount to get the sale, just like the girls did for Reginald when he bought a lot of shirts. But make sure you don't sell an item for less than it costs to make it, like Harriet did! Decide the lowest price you are willing to sell for *before* you start to negotiate.

★ You may have heard the saying, *It takes money to make money.* Sometimes you need money to buy the things you need to start your business. If so, you can ask your customers for money in advance as a deposit and use that money to start your business or place your first order. You can even give a discount to customers who give you a deposit, like the Startup Squad did when they offered a 15 percent discount on T-shirts if people paid in advance.

★ Negotiations don't have to always be about price. You can also exchange your products for something other than money. Especially when you're first starting out, you can save money by exchanging your product for something else you need, like supplies or advertising. Mo was willing to loan a guitar to the Radical Skinks as long as she got free publicity about her store and a guarantee for a future sale.

Customer Service is how you treat people before, during, and after they buy your products. It's important that your customers have a good experience so they will not only come back, but tell their friends to buy from you, too!

👍 Customer Service Tips

★ There's a saying that a happy customer will tell three people about their love for your business, but an unhappy consumer will tell ten people about their bad experience. Always try to leave customers with a good impression and make them feel special, even if they don't end up buying anything. Remember all the bad things Eleanor heard about the girls' customer service? And she wasn't even at the concert!

★ A little extra effort can create very loyal customers. Eleanor exchanged her customer's "warm" ice cream and his family became regular customers. If a bug lands in someone's lemonade, replace it. If someone drops their cookie or brownie, give them a new one. It will cost you a little extra money, but it will help create happy and loyal customers. And you'll end up making more money in the end.

★ A smile and a positive attitude make customers feel welcome and can help your business stand out from the competition. Try to remember Val's smile or Eleanor's "So sorry about that" line when you're dealing with a difficult customer. You can turn an unhappy customer into a happy one, who might even become a loyal customer for life.

Want our favorite recipe for lemonade and more tips about running your business? All that and more can be found in the first book in The Startup Squad series. You can read about how the girls first met and became friends, their misadventures running a lemonade stand, and what they learned about marketing, sales, location, and merchandising.

And you can learn more about running your own business at thestartupsquad.com and start planning your empire. Because GIRLS MEAN BUSINESS!

For help with these business tips, special thanks to Daniel R. Ames, Professor, Columbia Business School; Hafize Gaye Erkan, President, First Republic Bank; and Kathy Waller, former Chief Financial Officer, The Coca-Cola Company.

Earrings by Emma

Meet a real-life girl entrepreneur!

Four Twigs Photography

Emma Shelton has her own business, Earrings by Emma (EarringsByEmma.com), and she's the winner of the second Girls Mean Business contest.

Q: Tell us about your business.

A: My business makes and sells hypoallergenic plastic post earrings for sensitive ears of all ages.

Q: How old were you when you started, and where did your idea come from?

A: I started Earrings by Emma when I was eight years old. Since I had a hard time finding earrings that wouldn't irritate my sensitive ears, I started making my own. I quickly discovered that many others struggle with sensitive ears too. I have always wanted to start my own business, so this became a great opportunity for me to give it a try.

Q: What are the most fun parts of running a business?

A: The most fun parts of running a business are making money, meeting new people, and being able to meet a need for those with sensitive ears.

Q: What's the hardest?

A: The hardest part of running a business is working long days.

Q: What are your future plans for your business?

A: I hope to exponentially grow my online sales and continue to improve my business skills.

Q: What tasks take up the most time to run your business?

A: The tasks that take up the most time to run my business are preparing for and working trade shows, and inventory management, as we have a massive selection of earrings!

Q: Do you have a role model or mentor?

A: My dad and mom are great mentors. They are naturally entrepreneurial, so I have learned so much from watching them.

Q: What was the biggest mistake you made? What did you learn from it?

A: The biggest mistake I made was selling my earrings at an outdoor event. It was so windy that my earrings blew all over an Oklahoma farm! I learned that not all venues are appropriate for selling my products.

Q: What do you like to do when you're not conquering the business world?

A: When I am not conquering the business world, I enjoy drawing anime and spending time with my friends.

Q: Any advice for other girls starting a business?

A: My advice is to find a market that isn't being served and serve it—or find a need or a problem that hasn't been solved and innovate a new product or solution.

Want to learn about other girl entrepreneurs?
Go to thestartupsquad.com!

About the Authors

Brian Weisfeld has been building businesses his entire life. In elementary school, he bought ninety-five pounds of gummy bears and hired his friends to sell them. As a teen, he made and sold mixtapes (ask your parents what those are), sorted baseball cards (he got paid in cards), babysat four days a week after school, and sold nuts and dried fruit (and more gummy bears) in a neighborhood store. As an adult, Brian helped build a number of well-known billion-dollar companies, including IMAX Corporation and Coupons.com. Brian is the founder and Chief Squad Officer of The Startup Squad, an initiative that empowers girls to realize their potential and follow their dreams, whatever their passions. Brian lives in Silicon Valley and can often be found eating gummy bears with his wife while watching his two daughters sell lemonade from the end of their driveway.

Nicole C. Kear grew up in New York City, where she still lives with her husband as well as her three kids, who are budding lemonade moguls. She's written lots of essays and a memoir, *Now I See You*, for grown-ups, and the Fix-It Friends series for kids. She has a bunch of fancy, boring diplomas and one red clown nose from circus school. Seriously.

Learn more about real-life girl entrepreneurs like Emma at thestartupsquad.com!